yours truly,
LUCY B. PARKER
girl vs. superstar

"So who is this guy you've been going out with?" I asked. I still couldn't believe Mom had been hiding all this from me. Or that she had been able to hide it from me, because I'm really good at figuring that stuff out.

"It's . . . Alan Moses," she finally said.

Now I understood why she had hidden it from me. "You've been going out with Laurel Moses's father?!" I yelled. "After everything I went through with the Hat Incident?!"

Barbara was so startled she let the bra strap snap me so hard on the shoulder I yelped. "Laurel Moses, from *The World According to Madison Tennyson*?" she gasped. "My granddaughter and I just love that show!" Laurel Moses was one of the most famous people in the world. Even though she was only fourteen and her TV series was on Kidz TV, adults knew who she was because she sang and acted in movies, too.

Yeah, most people loved her, but me, Lucy B. Parker? I hated her.

yours truly,
LUCY B.
PARKER

girl
vs.
superstar

ROBIN PALMER

PUFFIN BOOKS
An Imprint of Penguin Group (USA) Inc.

PUFFIN BOOKS
Published by the Penguin Group
Penguin Young Readers Group, 345 Hudson Street,
New York, New York 10014, U.S.A.
Penguin Group (Canada), 90 Eglinton Avenue East, Suite 700, Toronto,
Ontario, Canada M4P 2Y3 (a division of Pearson Penguin Canada Inc.)
Penguin Books Ltd, 80 Strand, London WC2R 0RL, England
Penguin Ireland, 25 St Stephen's Green, Dublin 2, Ireland
(a division of Penguin Books Ltd)
Penguin Group (Australia), 250 Camberwell Road, Camberwell,
Victoria 3124, Australia (a division of Pearson Australia Group Pty Ltd)
Penguin Books India Pvt Ltd, 11 Community Centre,
Panchsheel Park, New Delhi - 110 017, India
Penguin Group (NZ), 67 Apollo Drive, Rosedale,
North Shore 0632, New Zealand (a division of Pearson New Zealand Ltd.)
Penguin Books (South Africa) (Pty) Ltd, 24 Sturdee Avenue,
Rosebank, Johannesburg 2196, South Africa

Registered Offices: Penguin Books Ltd, 80 Strand,
London WC2R 0RL, England

First published in the United States of America by Puffin Books and
G. P. Putnam's Sons, divisions of Penguin Young Readers Group, 2010

1 3 5 7 9 10 8 6 4 2

Library of Congress Cataloging-in-Publication Data is available

Puffin Books ISBN 978-0-14-241500-9

Printed in the United States of America

To Judy Blume, who gave me the precious gift
of feeling understood all those years ago…and
inspires me on a daily basis to attempt
to pay that forward.

Acknowledgments

For Jennifer Bonnell ... there are not enough super-latives in the "amazing/awesome/incredible" division of the English language to describe my gratitude, respect, and adoration of you and your talents as an editor and a person. Like Ms. Blume, you just "get" me ... and, more importantly, you "get" Lucy ... and I thank you from the bottom of my heart for this.

For Eileen Kreit, Kristin Gilson, Kristin Smith, and all the other goddesses at Puffin ... your support and belief in me, and your ability to transmit Lucy's Lucyness to the world is a dream come true. There isn't a writer in the world who has it as good as I do.

For Kate Lee ... who, as the best agent in the world, not only makes my life easy by taking care of all those icky business-y things for me, but also reminds me of the big picture on the days that I get stuck in the small one.

chapter 1

Dear Dr. Maude,

I know we don't actually know each other, but I know who you are from TV, which is kind of like knowing you. Especially since, before my parents got divorced, my dad convinced my mom to get a 46-inch TV screen, so now you're almost life-size when I watch you on your show. I have *Come On, People—Get with the Program* on pretty much any afternoon after school that I don't hang out with my sort-of friend Marissa, and listen to her talk nonstop. She's basically my only friend ever since I got friend-dumped right before sixth grade started.

I got your e-mail address off your website (BTW that picture of you with your two dachshunds is sooooooo cute!! I love dogs, too, but my mom's allergic to them. That's why I only have a cat. But when I grow up I'm totally getting a dog). I know how busy you are, so I won't go into all of it now, because it's kind of a long story, but let's just say that between being friend-dumped, and having my mother bug me nonstop about how it's time for me to start wearing a bra, and the Hat Incident, sixth grade is NOT what I was hoping it would be. In fact, it feels like it just gets worse and worse every day.

Anyway, I was wondering if you might have some advice

1

for a person with these types of problems. And please don't say, "Don't worry, Lucy, everything changes if you wait long enough," because that's what my dad keeps saying to me. And, frankly, I find it REALLY ANNOYING.

I look forward to hearing from you.

yours truly,
LUCY B. Parker

Obviously I sent that e-mail to Dr. Maude too soon. If I had waited until after that Wednesday evening in January when Mom took me to the Holyoke Mall, I would have had a lot more advice to ask Dr. Maude.

I should have known something was wrong the minute Mom asked me if I wanted to go. We barely ever went to the mall on a school night, even though, if it were up to me, I'd go there every day because both H&M and Target are there, and they're my two favorite stores in the entire world.

"You want to stop at Scoops for some ice cream first?" Mom asked as we got into Virginia Woolf, our twenty-year-old blue Volvo. I don't know why our car couldn't have a normal name—like, say, Christine, which is what my ex–best friend Rachel's mother's car is called—instead of being named after some famous writer, especially one who walked into a river and drowned herself, but both my parents are weird that way. Dad's red Saab was

2

named Alfred Stieglitz after a famous photographer, which is an even weirder name than Virginia Woolf. And almost impossible to spell, even for someone like me, who was runner-up in the Jefferson Middle School Spelling Bee this year after Danica Morris (I totally knew how to spell *philistine*, but I was so nervous during the bee that I spelled it *p-h-i-l-e* instead of *i*). Dad's always saying that "creative types" (Mom's a writer and Dad's a photographer) are allowed to be a little weird, but I'm sorry—lately? They've both been a lot weird.

The minute Mom said "ice cream" I definitely knew something was up. Ever since I turned twelve back in November, I was only supposed to have ice cream on the weekends, on account of the fact that the more sugar I ate, the more pimples popped up on my forehead, no matter how much zit cream I put on before I went to bed at night. Unless it was a super-special occasion during the week—like after a chorus concert (even though I was only a mouther instead of a singer because my voice isn't very good). Dad's girlfriend, Sarah—who isn't creative-weird, but just weird-weird because she's a yoga teacher—gave me a bottle of this essential oil and said that if I dabbed a few drops on my wrists and behind my ears, it would make it so that I don't want sugar, but I never use it because I think it makes me smell like a sweaty sneaker. The last thing I needed after the Hat Incident was for people in Northampton to start going around saying, "Lucy B. Parker smells like a sweaty sneaker."

"Okay, what's going on?" I demanded as I finished the last bite of my mint-chocolate-chip butterscotch sundae (another clue something weird was going on—usually I was allowed to get only one scoop) as we walked into the mall.

Mom flashed me another big smile, the third one in the last half hour. That was another thing: over the last few months, Mom had been a lot happier than usual. Like singing-out-loud-as-she-made-dinner-even-though-she-had-a-horrible-voice-too kind of happy. It wasn't like she had spent every night crying since she and Dad had gotten divorced the year before, like her BFF Deanna had done when she got divorced, but she definitely hadn't been singing.

Right before we got on the escalator I stopped short. Suddenly, it all made sense. "Nope. I'm not going," I announced.

"What are you talking about, honey?" Mom asked all innocently. "We're going to Target. You love Target."

My eyes narrowed. "But you're not taking me to Target—you're taking me to Barbara's Bra World." Which just happened to be next to Target. I bet the mall people did that on purpose so that people like me would think they were going to their favorite store, but really were being tricked into something even more horrible than getting a cavity filled or having a mixed-fractions pop quiz: bra shopping.

If there's anything I hate more than mixed fractions,

it's my boobs. Seventh graders like Frankie Bankuti and Timmy McFarland stare at them, but even worse than that is the fact that it makes it hard to read the writing on my green I DON'T PLAY WELL WITH OTHERS T-shirt because some of the letters are on top of my boobs and some are underneath. (Sarah's always saying that wearing a T-shirt like that is putting out a "negative vibe" because, unlike someone like, say, Nicole Meloni, I actually do play well with others—but that's because Sarah barely thinks anything's funny.) Ever since the week before sixth grade started, when I woke up one morning to find that I had gone from totally flat chested to having two large hacky sacks on my chest, Mom's been on me to start wearing a bra. I keep refusing, even though at Christmastime she tried to bribe me by saying she'd give me twenty dollars if I did. The one time I tried one on, it was so itchy that I got a rash and had to put calamine lotion on my chest and I used too much and it ruined my Maggie Simpson T-shirt.

Back when Rachel and Missy (my other ex-BFF) and I would go to the mall on Saturdays, before they frienddumped me three days before sixth grade started, they loved to try on bras in Forever 21, even though they barely had anything to put in them. (While they did that, I spent my time trying on barrettes and headbands, but that was before the Straightening Iron Incident.) My sortof friend Marissa who is almost completely flat has been using every birthday and penny-in-the-mall-fountain wish since she was nine to ask for big boobs. She actually cuts ads out of the Macy's circular of bras she wants and keeps them on the bulletin board above her desk, which, if you ask me, is beyond weird. I call Marissa my "sort-of" friend because there's no way I could ever be BFFs with someone so annoying, even though she totally thinks we are. To be honest, the only reason we started hanging out is because my last name is Parker and hers is Parini, which means she sits right in front of me in homeroom. I was so nervous about not having anyone to eat lunch with that first day of sixth grade because of the Rachel/Missy thing that I just asked Marissa, and now she won't leave me alone. I have to listen to her go on and on about horses, and all the different things she's allergic to, and the dolls from different countries she collects. Seriously, I'm surprised people don't literally die from boredom after being around her.

Mom grabbed my hand and yanked me on the escalator. "We're going to Target. I promise." She reached into her purse and took out a crumpled-up list that had a coffee stain on it. "I have a list and everything." That was another clue something was going on because although Mom made tons of lists, she always lost them right away.

Once we got inside Target, the sigh of relief I let out was so loud that Mom said, "Lucy, is that really necessary?" Then she turned to me. "Go get those Converses you want and meet me over near the cleaning supplies."

"Really?" I'm totally addicted to Converses. I have

five pairs of high-tops and three pairs of low-tops. Not only do I have them in all different colors like purple (my favorite color) and red (my second favorite), but I also have them in tie-dye (Dad got them for me for my twelfth birthday even though they were pretty expensive). Mom and I had a deal that I could get a pair of One Stars if I got an 85 on my mixed-fractions test. I had gotten only an 80, but if she didn't remember that, because she was being all weird, it's not like I was going to remind her.

She nodded. "I'll meet you near the paper towels in ten minutes," she said as she began to wheel her cart away, humming so loud off-key I thought I was going to die.

Something was going on. And I was going to find out what it was.

"Lucy, you do not need another box of maxipads," Mom said loudly at the checkout counter ten minutes later as I dumped a box of Always Maximum Protection Maxis on the belt along with the sneakers.

I cringed. As much as I loved my mom, she had a totally loud inside voice that seemed like it got even louder whenever we were talking about anything period- or bra-related.

"But this one has wings," I whispered. "It's important to have those." I wasn't sure why, but the announcer in the commercial made it seem like if they were missing, you were setting yourself up for big trouble, liked ruined underwear. Even though I still hadn't gotten my period yet, the last time I counted I had seven boxes of maxipads, minipads, and pantiliners in my closet so when the day came, I'd be prepared. For a while I was wearing a pad every day just to be safe, but then Mom yelled at me that we weren't made of money and made me stop. Now I just made sure never to leave the house without at least one of each in my knapsack.

Out of the fifty-three girls in the entire sixth grade, only twenty-two had gotten their periods so far, so it wasn't like I was behind schedule or anything. As long as I was the twenty-sixth to get mine, I was above average, which is all I cared about. As the Keeper of the Periods at Jefferson, I kept a notebook of who got theirs when, and everyone knew to come to me if they needed that information for some reason. It wasn't like it made me popular or anything (I was probably in the fortieth percentile of popularity), but after the Hat Incident, not only did everyone at Jefferson know who I was but probably everyone in the entire town of Northampton did. Maybe even Amherst, which was a few towns away.

I looked at all the cleaning supplies that were being rung up. "Is Grandma Maureen coming to visit?" I asked suspiciously. Our house wasn't dirty or anything, but the only time Mom did a humongous cleaning was when my grandmother came to visit.

"No," Mom replied. "But I thought on Friday we'd all come back to the house for dessert after dinner."

"Who's 'we'?"

Mom took a deep breath as we grabbed the bags and started walking out into the mall. "Well, for the last six weeks I've sort of been . . . seeing someone," she said nervously, "and we decided last week that the time has come for everyone to meet."

"What do you mean 'seeing someone'?" I asked.

"I mean . . . dating someone."

I stopped so short I almost fell on my butt. "You're dating someone?!" I cried. "I haven't heard you say anything to Deanna about that!" Deanna had been Mom's BFF ever since they were roommates their first year in college at Smith, which was just down the street from our house. Mom told her everything. And because I have super-strong hearing, sometimes when I'm upstairs in my room and they're in the kitchen having coffee, I just happen to overhear them. Okay, maybe sometimes I'm not in my room—maybe I'm at the top of the stairs—but I'm not eavesdropping. I'm overlistening. There's a difference.

I was so shocked and in such a total daze that my mom was dating that I didn't even realize we had ended up in the middle of Barbara's Bra World. "Wait a minute—not only are you telling me you have a boyfriend, but you're going to make me try on bras, too?!" I yelled. I couldn't believe how unfair my mother was being. Not to mention if she had known she was going to do this, the least she could have done was let me get a large sundae instead of a small one.

Before I knew it, I had been taken prisoner by Barbara, the owner, and had a tape measure around my chest. "So who is this person?" I demanded as I tried to squirm away. "Is it Liam from Coffee Corner?" Liam was a musician with long dreadlocks who had had a crush on Mom forever. He was nice and all—sometimes if Maia, the owner, wasn't there, he gave me and Marissa free coconut-peanut-butter cookies—but he had the worst B.O. on the planet, and there was no way I would be able to sit next to him for an entire dinner.

"No, it's not Liam," Mom said as she picked up a light blue bra that had so much padding it would've made me look like I was in eleventh grade.

I exhaled the breath I had been holding because Barbara smelled like a mixture of egg salad and very flowery perfume. "Then who is it?" I asked.

"Well, it's—" Mom began to say.

"Oh my God!" I gasped, pulling my purple knit newsboy cap down farther on my head in order to try to hide as two girls walked into the store. It was Lisa Silfen and Shelly Powell—the two most popular girls in the seventh grade. It wasn't like I knew them personally, on account of the fact that you had to be pretty popular yourself in order for the older popular kids to talk to you, but they definitely knew who I was because of the Hat Incident.

"What is it, dear?" asked Barbara loudly. "Am I pulling the tape measure too tight around your bosoms?"

Even though I didn't dare look over at the girls, I could hear one of them laugh. When I got to school tomorrow, I was going to ask Mr. Mackey, the science teacher, if you could actually die of embarrassment. That is, I'd ask him if it didn't happen to me before that.

"Honey, what's wrong?" Mom asked in her loud voice. "Your face is all red. Are you okay?" She felt my forehead. "Do you think you're coming down with something?"

"Can we just leave?" I whispered between gritted teeth.

"What, sweetie?" Mom said. "I can't understand you."

"I was right—34A!" Barbara announced. She flashed me a smile. "I knew that just by looking at you!" She turned to Mom. "This one's going to be very bosomy when she gets older, though. Believe me, when you've been in this business as long as I have, you know these things."

If no one had died of embarrassment before this moment, I was pretty sure I was about to be the first one.

Barbara clapped her hands. "Okay, into the dressing room!" she ordered.

I think I ran faster than I ever had in my entire life. And for someone who hates exercise so much that she carries around a note that says, "Please excuse Lucy B. Parker from gym today on account of the fact that she is menstruating," that was saying a lot. (When Marissa helped me write the note, and before she forged Mom's signature by studying her real signature from a field-trip permission slip, she said that "menstruating" was better than "has her period" because it made it sound more official.) Luckily, when I peered out, I saw Lisa and Shelly leaving. If they had come into the dressing room area to try on bras as well, I definitely would have had to die.

Instead, Mom and Barbara came in, which was almost as in bad. Then they both came into the actual dressing room, which was even worse.

"What are you doing?" I asked them.

"Well, we have to make sure your bosoms are properly supported in the brassiere, dear," said Barbara, who was stinking up the whole room with her perfume.

"Take off your shirt, honey," said Mom.

I crossed my arms over my chest. Yup, this was definitely the most embarrassing moment of my life. Even worse than the Hat Incident.

"Why?" I asked.

"Because I'm your mother, and I said so," she replied firmly. "And because if you do, I'll take you to H&M after this and let you get a hat."

As I took off my shirt, I closed my eyes and kept them closed the entire time. It was bad enough that my mother could see my bare boobs, but a complete stranger who wasn't even a doctor was looking at them, too?!

Barbara must have been psychic because right then she said, "There's no need to be embarrassed, dear—I've seen more boobies in my life than you'd ever imagine!"

I cringed. Bosoms, boobies—why could she just call them boobs?! Or at least just breasts, like Ms. DeMarco, my health teacher, did?

"Now in you go," she said, holding out the bra.

I shoved my arms in it. "Okay, it fits—can we just buy it and get out of here?" I asked as she fastened it in the back.

"Now you have to position yourself in it," Barbara explained. "So reach in and lift your bosoms up—"

Could this get any worse? But I knew that if I didn't do it myself, she'd probably reach in and do it, which would be just beyond awful. "So who is this guy you've been going out with?" I asked as I did what I was told. I still couldn't believe Mom had been hiding all this from me. Or that she had been able to hide it from me, because I'm really good at figuring that stuff out. Since the divorce, she said she didn't want to date and instead had been spending all her time writing her novel. But that hadn't been going so well because she had what she calls "writer's block," where basically she does anything but write—like polish her nails or organize her sock drawer.

"It's... Alan Moses," she finally said.

Now I understood why she had hidden it from me. "You've been going out with Laurel Moses's father?!" I yelled. "After everything I went through with the Hat Incident?!"

Barbara was so startled she let the bra strap snap me so hard on the shoulder I yelped. "Laurel Moses, from *The World According to Madison Tennyson*?" she gasped. "My granddaughter and I just love that show!" Laurel

13

Moses was one of the most famous people in the world. Even though she was only fourteen and her TV series was on Kidz TV, adults knew who she was because she sang and acted in movies, too.

Yeah, most people loved her, but me, Lucy B. Parker? I hated her.

chapter 2

Dear Dr. Maude,

I am using my mom's iPhone to type this, so there might be some typos. I know you haven't written back to my other e-mail yet, but I just had to write to you because I just got some AWFUL, AWFUL news. It's too long of a story to type on an iPhone, but I just found out that my MOTHER has, without me knowing it, been dating Laurel Moses's FATHER.

Yes, THE Laurel Moses, the famous superstar, who you might actually know personally because Marissa says all famous people know each other.

I can't go into it now, but Laurel is the person behind the Hat Incident and one of the main reasons why my life is so horrible at the moment. And now I have to sit through dinner with her as well? I'm sure you agree that that's JUST TOTALLY NOT FAIR.

If you have any advice as to what to do after finding out that your mother has been dating the father of your archenemy, I'd really appreciate it.

yours truly,
LUCY B. PARKER

Dad says that *hate* is a very strong word and that if you can use *strongly dislike* that's a lot better because it will help your karma, which is something that the Buddhists—which is the religion he and Mom practice—believes in. It's not the kind of religion where you go to church or temple on a weekly basis—it's more about sitting on a pillow on the floor with your eyes closed and meditating (which, according to him, means trying not to think). Anyway, Dad says that when someone makes you mad or annoys you, you should put yourself in her shoes and try to think about why she might be acting that way, but because Laurel is like the most popular person in the world, I couldn't even begin to imagine what it would be like to wear her shoes. Especially because I doubt she wears Converses—she probably wears super-expensive high heels, which are something I will never wear in my life. I'm what Dad calls coordination-challenged.

But sometimes *hate* is the only word for what you feel, and if you had been totally humiliated in front of the entire town where you had lived for all of your twelve years on the planet, you'd probably hate the person responsible for that, too.

But before there was the Hat Incident, there was the Straightening Iron Incident, which is why I had to start wearing hats in the first place.

What happened was that I thought it would be a good idea to start sixth grade with a more grown-up look—especially since, when Rachel and Missy called me to friend-dump me, they said the main reason was that they thought I was sort of tomboyish because I had no interest in wearing a bra, wore Converses almost every day (unless I was wearing flip-flops in the summer), didn't have any interest in makeup, and didn't have a crush on anyone. I tried to tell them that (a) not only were those really stupid reasons to dump someone, especially because all the reality shows on MTV make it seem like if you have a crush, and that crush turns into your boyfriend, you end up spending most of your time crying instead of having fun—especially when he breaks up with you, but (b) I never went anywhere without my Smith's Rosebud Salve Strawberry Lip Balm, which, while not exactly a lipstick, did make my lips look a little more pink, not to mention smells really good, and that was kind of like wearing makeup. But they dumped me anyway. And then I cried so hard for so long and got such a bad headache that I had to take two of Mom's Advil.

So the day after they dumped me—two days before school started—I decided that maybe if I used Mom's straightening iron and got rid of my frizzy-not-curly brown curls, maybe they'd change their minds and like me again. Mom was at her writer's group that afternoon, so she wasn't around to show me how to use it. But if she had been, she probably would've told me that putting the iron around my entire left pigtail and leaving it there for an entire half-hour episode of *Animal Police 911* wasn't a smart thing to do. See, I figured the longer I kept it there, the straighter it would get. But that's not what happened. What happened was I ended up burning the pigtail so badly that most of it just crumbled and fell off. The good news is that I didn't bother trying to iron the other one, so only half my hair was gone instead of all of it. The bad news was that I looked lopsided, like the papier-mâché Easter egg I made in first grade that Mom keeps on what I call her "Ugly Things Lucy Has Made in School over the Years but I Love Them Anyway" shelf in her office in the attic.

When Mom came home, she freaked out and immediately drove me over to Deanna's house so she could fix my hair, because Deanna's a hairdresser, with her own salon and everything. The problem was, she had to cut it really, really short, which left me looking like a giant egg with ears, which is why I wore my Boston Red Sox cap on the first day of school and have been wearing hats every day since. At first no one said anything, because it's not like wearing a hat is all that weird, especially a Red Sox cap because we live in Massachusetts. But when a person wears a hat every single day—and not just baseball caps, but purple knit newsboy caps and red cowboy hats and black berets (according to Mom, they're very French, and she would know because she lived in Paris for a while during college)—then other people start to talk. All these rumors started about why I was wearing hats—things like I was so upset when Rachel and Missy friend-dumped me that I shaved off all my hair, or I had cancer and had lost it all because of chemotherapy, like Michael Duarte's mother—but whenever someone asked, I just shrugged and said, "I just like wearing hats." It wasn't a total lie, although on Indian summer days my head did get pretty sweaty.

Marissa was totally annoying about the whole thing and kept saying, "Pleasepleaseplease, just tell me the real reason you wear hats. Because we're BFFs; you can tell me and I won't tell ANYONE, I SWEAR!" That wasn't true for two reasons: (a) Marissa has the biggest mouth in all of Jefferson Middle School and probably couldn't keep a secret even if someone offered her a million dollars, and (b) we're totally not BFFs and never will be. I told her that second part—not the "never will be" part, because that would've been really mean. But I did say that you had to be friends with someone for a pretty long time before you could officially call her your BFF, and that ever since being dumped, I didn't have any BFFs.

Anyway, on the day of the Hat Incident, back in November, I was walking down State Street after my dental cleaning with my red velvet cupcake (my favorite food in the world) from Sweet Lady Jane when a stuffed-up voice behind me yelled, "Lucy! Hey, Lucy! Wait up!" I turned around to see Marissa running toward me, pumping her arms like she was running the six-hundred-yard dash. Because Marissa has Ronald McDonald red hair and was wearing a hot pink down jacket with a fake leopard fur collar, you couldn't miss her.

"Omigod, omigod!" she panted when she caught up with me. "I'm so glad I found you because you're never, ever, ever going to believe who's inside the Tattered Cover right this very second."

The Tattered Cover was one of the many bookstores in the area. "People who want to buy books?" I said.

"No. Laurel. Moses," she announced, her voice quivering.

I didn't watch Laurel's show a lot because it happened to be on at the same time as *The Real Tenth Graders of New Jersey*, but in the episodes I had seen (before I hated her, obviously) I actually thought she was a good actress, and I even laughed out loud a few times. Especially in the scenes where Madison—the character she plays—dressed up in different disguises to stalk whatever boy she had a crush on that week. That's what the show is about—a girl who's boy-crazy.

Marissa, on the other hand, was completely obsessed with Laurel. Not only had she seen every episode of the show, but she owned every one of Laurel's movies on DVD (there were five), and every time a new online fan club was started, she signed up for it. Plus, she wore her Madison Tennyson T-shirt to school, which is a total fourth-grade thing to do.

The reason Laurel Moses was in Northampton was because she was shooting a movie about a girl in the old days who pretends to be a boy so she can play football. If you asked me, it sounded like a really boring movie, and I thought that before the Hat Incident even happened. Although rumor had it that Laurel had been in town for a week already, no one had seen her—not even Marissa, who had been hanging out outside the Hotel Northampton every day after school like a total stalker.

I don't know what I expected a movie set to be like, but this one sure was boring. Just a bunch of wires and trucks and people sitting around doing nothing except talking on cell phones or texting. Or, in the case of one guy, picking his nose when he thought no one was looking. But when the door of one of the RV trailers down the street opened and three people walked out, all the movie people started buzzing around.

Marissa started rocking back and forth. "Ohhh myyyy God," she moaned. Could she be more embarrassing? I took a step away from her, hoping no one would think I was with her. "There she is!" she screeched.

In between a bald guy who was messing with her hair and a nose-pierced woman was Laurel Moses. On TV she always dressed in cool clothes, with her long blonde hair looking super-pretty and straight (I wondered if she had to use a straightening iron or if hers was just naturally like that), but that day it was in braids and she was wearing overalls. She looked like one of Marissa's American Girl dolls (I would've said that before I hated her). Once she got in front of the bookstore, a guy wearing a Mickey Mouse T-shirt, jeans, and red Converse high-tops came rushing toward her and kissed her on both cheeks as he said, "Laurel! Dude! You look a-maz-ing!"

It was then that all the trouble started.

Because after he was done saying hello to her, he started freaking out about the fact that she didn't have a hat, saying things like, "I cannot shoot this scene without her wearing the hat! The hat is a character!" It's not like they taught us about movies in school (I wish they had because it would've been a lot more interesting than mixed fractions), but I knew enough to know that a hat couldn't be a character because it didn't talk, so I had no idea what this guy was going on about. Then this lady came running out of one of the RVs carrying a bunch of hats, but every time she held one up for him to see, he shook his head really hard. He was being such a jerk that the lady started to cry while Laurel just stood there staring at the ground. I happened to have some tissues in my jacket pocket (even though it had been four months since the friend-dumping, sometimes I still got really upset about it and would start to cry) and was thinking about whether I should cross the street and offer the woman one, when Mr. Mickey Mouse stopped yelling at her and pointed in my direction and yelled, "You in the hat!"

I looked around, but no one else was wearing a hat. When he said, "Yeah, you in the red-and-black-plaid newsboy cap. Get over here!" I definitely knew he meant me. Everyone was looking at me, and I thought about turning around and running as fast as I could, but then

I realized that having people say, "Lucy B. Parker ran away from the movie set," would be just as bad as, "Lucy B. Parker smells like a sweaty sneaker." As I crossed the street, I hoped that no one could see that my teeth were chattering, which they tend to do when I'm nervous. But then they really started getting loud when the guy reached over and yanked my hat right off my head in front of half of Northampton. Okay, maybe not half, but, still, there were a lot of people there. It was just as embarrassing if not more than having to take my shirt off in the dressing room in front of Mom and Barbara from Barbara's Bra World, but I didn't know that yet, seeing as that wouldn't happen for another two months. But I did know that it was so embarrassing that I was afraid it had brought on my period, which is why I was very glad I was wearing a maxipad.

Then, to make things twenty times worse, as I was standing there clutching at my egg-looking head in hopes that all the people staring at me with their mouths in the shape of Cheerios wouldn't actually notice that my head looked like an egg (including Rachel and Missy), I heard Marissa yell, "Holy moly! Now I know why you wouldn't show me your haircut!" It's things like that that explain why no one wants to be Marissa's friend.

Okay, so Laurel Moses wasn't the one who actually took my hat off my head, but what she did was way worse. When Mr. Mickey Mouse put the hat on her head, she started freaking out and batting it away like it was a bird that had just pooped on her and said, "Eww! Get that thing off me right now!"

Thing?! It wasn't a thing. It was my hat. Maybe it hadn't cost a hundred dollars, but it wasn't like I had gotten it for fifty cents at Goodwill. It was from H&M and it cost $14.98, which isn't exactly cheap.

Mr. Mickey Mouse started to explain to her that this was exactly the kind of a hat that a girl in 1957 who was trying to disguise herself as a boy in order to get on the football team would wear, but she cut him off and said the thing that totally made me hate her:

She said, "But what if there's lice in it?"

I couldn't believe it.

Everyone knew that accusing someone of having lice was even worse than telling her she had B.O., or that her breath stank. Even if you were a ginormous star who had been an actress from the time you were six and got to ride in limousines and go to the MTV Movie Awards, you had to know that. And not only that, but Laurel Moses said it in front of my entire town. She may have been the most popular girl in the world, but she didn't have the right to go around spreading lies and hurting people's feelings. Because I totally DID NOT have lice. And to make it worse, now that my hat was off my head, anyone who wasn't blind could see that I barely had any hair left!

Then Laurel yanked my hat off her head and threw it on the ground, where it landed in a puddle, and huffed,

"I'm calling my agent!" before stomping off toward her trailer with the bald guy and nose-pierced girl trailing behind her. I thought Mr. Mickey Mouse would apologize to me, but he didn't. Instead, he just ran after them, calling, "Laurel, honey, sweetie, just hold up a moment, okay?"

Having Laurel Moses accuse me of having lice wasn't even the worst part. The worst part was hearing the giggles that started when I squatted down to get my hat out of the puddle. Most people know what it's like to feel their face get all hot when they get embarrassed, but very few people (other than bald men like my uncle Steve) know what it's like to have their entire head feel like it's on fire, which is what happened to me when everyone laughed at me. At first the giggles were on the quiet side, but then they got louder. The part that was even worse-than-the-worst-part was when, without even turning around, I could tell that the loudest laughs of them all were coming from Rachel and Missy. My ex-friends. Whose giggles I would've recognized anywhere because that's what happens when you're friends with people since kindergarten.

So that's why I hated Laurel Moses.

And that, if you asked me, was a perfectly acceptable reason.

chapter 3

Dear Dr. Maude,

My mom stepped out to go to the bathroom (this bra shopping thing is taking a lot longer than we expected). Even though I don't know if you wrote back to my last e-mail because I can't check my account on Mom's phone, I thought I would just send you another one. If you haven't written back yet with some advice, please, please, PLEASE do so now because I really need it.

Thanks very much.

yours truly,
Lucy B. Parker

When your mother has just told you she's been dating your archenemy's father, the good news is that you're too shocked to keep being embarrassed about the fact that some total stranger who smells like egg salad and bad perfume has her hands inside what's about to become your first bra.

In fact, I was so shocked, I couldn't think of anything to say at all—which for someone whose "Additional

Comments" section of her report card always says something like, "While Lucy's running commentary is very entertaining, she would do well to learn to listen more and talk less," is a big deal.

Luckily, I didn't have to because, while I stood there shivering in my bra with the straps that were digging into my shoulders, Mom told me (and Barbara) the story of how she and Alan got together.

Obviously I knew that Mom knew Laurel, because she was tutoring her. A few days after the Hat Incident, Mom sat me down and said, "I know you're not going to like the idea, but Donna at Two Cups of Joe gave Laurel Moses's father my number because Laurel needs a tutor while she's here, and he called and I said yes because he's going to pay me three times my normal hourly rate." Because she always had writer's block and couldn't finish her novel, the way Mom made money was by tutoring. I told her she was wrong—it wasn't like I didn't like the idea . . . I hated it—but she said that was too bad and that as long as she was paying for my Converses, I didn't have a say in the matter. Usually, she had the kids she tutored come over to the house, but in this case she'd do it at the Hotel Northampton or in Laurel's trailer on the set so that I didn't have to cross paths with her, which made me feel a little bit better. Then Mom said that when she got her first check from Laurel's father, she'd use part of it to buy me the Emily the Strange tote bag I had been begging her for from Faces, which made me feel a lot better.

I knew that if Marissa found out, she'd blab it to the entire school and kids would be coming up to me every day saying, "So what's Laurel Moses really like?"—maybe even Rachel and Missy, because even though they had dumped me, they were huge fans and would have wanted to know stuff like whether Laurel Moses's hair looked as good in person as it did on TV or whether it was all strawlike. And I wouldn't be able to answer because (a) I wouldn't have been anywhere near her and (b) the last thing I wanted was to be the center of attention again at school like I was the day after the Hat Incident. Thanks to Whitney Thomas's super-fancy cell-phone camera and her Facebook page—there was a picture of me looking all bug-eyed and clutching at my head in hopes of hiding my almost-baldness, which was almost as bad as the Hat Incident itself. Mrs. Riley, our principal, made Whitney take it down the same day she'd posted it, but that didn't happen until third period, after I had already run to the bathroom twice and locked myself in the handicapped stall to cry. And it didn't stop David Murray from whispering, "So the *B* in Lucy B. Parker is for Baldy, huh?" when Mrs. Kline called me up to the board the next day to add $7^3/_4$ and $6^7/_8$. (Which, BTW, I got wrong. I was bad enough at mixed fractions when things were going okay, let alone when I was totally humiliated.)

But because Marissa has this way of knowing when you're keeping a secret and won't leave you alone until you tell her what it is, I told her. And of course by the time school was out that day, everyone at Jefferson knew—even the eighth graders. I overheard one of them say, "Hey, that's that bald sixth grader whose mother is Laurel Moses's tutor," as I walked to the bus.

Sure enough, after that, almost every day at least one kid, if not more, would ask me questions about Laurel—stuff like, "What's her favorite candy?" and "Do you happen to know what her favorite Wii game is?"—even though I kept saying, "I have no idea because I've never been near her other than one time at the bookstore." Rachel and Missy didn't come up to me, but at one point during gym it looked like they were going to. That made me feel like I was going to throw up because I was both super-excited and super-scared at the same time, kind of like what happens when you ride a big roller coaster.

But if I did want to know anything about Laurel, I could've just asked Mom because from the very first day she tutored her it was like they were total BFFs. "Laurel has such a great sense of humor!" Mom said one night as we ate Indian food. "I can't believe that Laurel is fluent in French!" she said the following week as we ate Mexican food. "I'm just so impressed by how polite and well mannered Laurel is!" she said as we ate Tibetan food the next week. Seriously, the way she talked about her you'd think she liked her more than me, her own daughter.

"Okay, I'm putting an embargo on this subject," I said the next time she brought her up; in Costco, as I threw a jumbo box of Kotex Lightdays Pantiliners (105 count!) in the cart. *Embargo* was one of our vocab words that week, and it meant "a restraint or hindrance; prohibition," or, in plain English, "Don't bring it up again or ELSE."

"Honey, I know you're still upset about the hat," Mom said as she took the pantiliners out and put them back on the shelf, "but I'm telling you, I think you'd really like her if you got to know her."

"Well, I'm not going to get to know her," I said, reaching for the box and throwing it back in again, "because I'm never going to be in the same room with her if I can help it."

"You never know. You might be," Mom said softly.

When you think about it, it's a very weird comment. But that day, in the middle of Costco—my third favorite store after Target and H&M (how could a person not love a place where almost everything is king-size or a multipack?)—I was too busy thinking about all the things I would've bought had I not recently spent all my saved-up allowance on the entire seven-book set of the Harry Potter series with the new covers.

It turned out that every time Laurel's dad, Alan, would come to pick Laurel up at the end of tutoring, he and Mom would talk for a few minutes. At first it was just about Laurel and how she was doing in her schoolwork. (According to Mom, she was a great student, and even though she was technically in ninth grade, she was reading books that twelfth graders read. Of course she was—she was Laurel Moses, the most perfect girl in

America!) But then the talks started to get longer and non-Laurel-related, and then one day Alan asked her if she'd be interested in having coffee sometime. And Mom said yes. They had such a nice time together they decided to do it a second time, and then a third time, and before they knew it they were having coffee almost every afternoon while I was at school and Laurel was shooting, talking about all sorts of stuff like movies and music and politics.

And then one Friday night when I was at Frankie's Pizzeria with Dad and Sarah (because that's how I spent my Friday nights now that I was no longer having sleepovers with Rachel and Missy—the one time I slept over Marissa's she spent the whole night giving me a tour of her dollhouse and telling me the entire history of every single piece of furniture in it, and I swore to myself to never, EVER do that again), she went to dinner with him at Chez Maurice. Which just happened to have been voted the Most Romantic Restaurant in Northampton three years in a row by the *Northampton Gazette*.

"And that's when our relationship moved to another level," Mom said as she held out another bra for me to try on. Luckily, Barbara had left the dressing room midstory to go help someone who actually wanted a bra.

"What do you mean by that?" I demanded.

"Well, that's when . . . he kissed me," she replied.

"Okay, I SO do not need to know that!" I yelled as I yanked the straps over my shoulders. But even worse than the idea of my mom kissing someone other than my father (even though they were divorced) was the idea that I hadn't known any of this. I wasn't a good singer, or a good dancer because of the coordination problem, but if there's one thing I'm great at, it's overlistening and figuring out things my parents are trying to hide from me. For instance, when my parents sat me down the year before and said, "We have something we need to discuss with you," I immediately said, "You're getting divorced, aren't you?" It totally shocked them because they thought they had been good about keeping it a secret. But when you wake up and find your father sleeping on the couch almost every night, you pretty much know something not so good is going on, even before trying to overlisten to their conversations.

"But why do you have to like him?" I asked as I adjusted my 34A boobs into the thing. "Why can't you like Liam instead?" The whole B.O. didn't seem so bad, not anymore. Plus, as far as I knew, he didn't have any kids. Let alone famous ones.

"Because we have a lot of things in common," Mom said as she stood back to get a look at me. "Oh honey . . . that looks so cute on you!" she said. Her eyes got all misty. "I can't believe my jelly bean is old enough to be wearing a bra. How did this happen?"

I rolled my eyes. "Um, maybe because everyone on the Parker side of the family has big boobs?" It was true—even though Mom's were on the smaller side, Dad's sister

Catherine's were huge. If mine ended up as big as hers, I was going to get a breast reduction, which is this operation that Marissa's mom got where they made them smaller. It really helped because before the operation she had such bad back problems she would have to stay in bed with a heating pad. "But you're changing the subject," I said.

"Well, first of all, he likes to do the *New York Times* crossword puzzle—"

"So? Dad does the crossword, too," I said as she did something to make the bra tighter. "He can even do it in pen because he barely ever screws up. Ouch!" I yelped. "My circulation is being cut off!"

"Enough with the dramatics, Lucy," Mom sighed as she moved the clasp to a different hook. "And we both like to play Scrabble—"

"Dad won first place in the Two Cups of Joe Scrabble tournament!" I retorted. I poked at my rib. "I think one of my ribs is broken."

"Lucy," Mom warned.

"Seriously. I think it is."

"You'll live," she said. She held out her hand. "Take that off and give it to me so I can go pay," she said.

I had to say, I was pretty impressed with how easily I unhooked the bra without even looking. That didn't mean I was going to wear the thing on a regular basis. "I'm sorry, but just because you have two things in common doesn't mean you should marry him!" I blurted out.

Mom took the bra from me. "Who said anything

about marriage? Now we're all going to dinner on Saturday, and that's that. End of discussion," she said firmly. She opened the dressing room door to leave, as I stood there almost completely naked for everyone to see my boobies or bosoms or breasts or whatever you wanted to call them.

"Fine," I said. I knew not to say anything more than that. On their own, "that's that" and "End of discussion" were bad enough, but both at the same time? Code for "If you bring it up again, no TV or Internet for two days."

She held one of the bras up. "And you better not 'forget' to wear this when we go," she warned.

I wondered if every girl's mother could read their minds, or just mine.

chapter 4

Dear Dr. Maude,

I'm sure you have a lot of people who write you saying, "Dr. Maude, I have a HUGE problem and I really need advice," but in my case, my problem really IS huge and I really DO need advice, which is why I was hoping you would've written me back by now.

We're about to leave to go have dinner with Laurel and her father, and I really REALLY don't want to go. Like to the point where I'd rather stay home and do my mixed-fractions homework, which, if you knew me, you'd know is one of the things I hate most in life. Anyway, I was going to say that you can't call me on my cell phone because it was taken away from me after Mom got last month's bill and saw that I had used it to text fifty-seven votes for the hairless Chihuahua on *America's Funniest Looking Pet*, but I was thinking that maybe you could call her cell phone and ask to speak to me. You don't even have to say it's you—you can just say it's "a friend," and I'll know who it is. Her number is 323-788-6868.

Thanks very much—I really appreciate it.

yours truly,
Lucy B. Parker

I wondered if, when introducing their daughter to the man she's been dating in secret and his famous daughter, every girl's mother says something really obvious like, "Lucy, this is Alan Moses and his daughter, Laurel."

As if there was a chance I wouldn't recognize Laurel Moses seeing that (a) she was the most famous teenager in America; (b) she was responsible for the most embarrassing moment of my life; and (c) all the other diners in Madame Wu's were staring at her.

I wanted to say, "Yeah, so?" but instead I mumbled, "Nice to meet you," because even though I often thought mean things, I very rarely said them out loud.

As I looked down at my boots, I noticed that Laurel was wearing boots, too. While mine were scuffed-up brown cowboy ones, hers were black and shiny with kind of high heels and probably cost like five hundred dollars. When Marissa had showed up at my house that afternoon to help me pick out an outfit (uninvited, I might add), I had told her that there was no way I was going out of my way to dress up for dinner (especially since her pick was this hideous pink dress stashed away in the back of my closet that Mom had made me wear to my cousin Mark's high school graduation the spring before). But the truth was after she (finally) left, I took my time to put together what I though was a great outfit. I was wearing my BOYS ARE STUPID, THROW ROCKS AT THEM T-shirt, a camel-colored cardigan, a dark purple wool miniskirt from H&M, rainbow tights, my boots, and the lilac angora beret that

Sarah had gotten me for my birthday. And—after Mom had ordered me back upstairs—my bra (which was so itchy I almost got the calamine lotion out again). In fact, it was such a good outfit that I had decided I'd wear it for my seventh-grade picture (maybe minus the hat if my hair had grown out by then). The only part of the outfit that I planned to leave out for sure was the pimple to the left of my nose. I had woken up with it that morning, and, thanks to the fact that I couldn't seem to stop touching it, it had gone from kind of big to ginormous.

Except now that I was standing in front of Laurel Moses—who, along with the boots, was wearing jeans (perfectly faded without any stains of any kind on them), a peach-colored silky shirt with cool butterfly sleeves that probably cost a thousand dollars, and no pimples— it no longer felt like such a good outfit. Instead, I felt like a box of crayons had exploded on my body.

"You, too," Laurel said, sounding as excited about this dinner as I felt. In her case, I'm sure it was because she was mad that she was missing out on whatever it was that big stars did on Saturday nights, like huge parties with all-you-can-eat sushi. Maybe even with Jackson Barber, another teen star who all the magazines said was her boyfriend.

"It's so great to meet you, Lucy!" Alan boomed as he thrust out his hand. "Your mom has told me so much about you!"

I guess I thought that with such a pretty and famous

daughter, Alan would be really handsome, but he wasn't. He wasn't ugly or anything, just really normal looking, like a dentist or something. He had what Dad called a "receding hairline" (Dad, on the other hand, had so much hair that he wore it in a ponytail), glasses, and a semi-big nose. As I shook his hand, I tried to keep a poker face because his hand was really clammy. Like gross clammy. But I didn't wipe it off on my skirt, even though I really wanted to.

"And I like your hat," Alan said. He turned to Laurel. "Laurel, isn't that a pretty hat?"

She nodded, but it wasn't an oh-my-God-yes-it's-so-pretty! nod—it was more like a no-it's-not-but-I'm-nodding-so-my-dad-doesn't-yell-at-me-later-for-being-rude nod.

I clamped it down on my head in case Laurel got any ideas. "Thank you," I said. I squinted—was that a drop of sweat rolling down Alan's face?

"Why don't we sit down and get the ordering out the way so you girls can have a nice chat," Mom said. "I have a feeling you're going to find you have a lot in common."

Laurel and I looked at each other. Her expression said exactly what I was thinking: *I kind of doubt it.*

At least we had that in common.

Thing number one Laurel and I didn't have in common? Food.

"I was thinking," Mom said after we were settled at the table, "instead of each of us ordering our own dishes, why don't we order family-style!" She didn't notice that the entire restaurant was still staring at us. Or, rather, at Laurel.

I choked on the crunchy noodles they gave you for free when you sat down. She was using the word *family* already?! If I still had my phone, I would've texted Marissa right then to double-check if that was a bad sign, but instead I was going to have to wait until I got home. Marissa was annoying, but she knew about this stuff. Her parents had gotten divorced when she was six, and then her mom had a bunch of boyfriends before she married her stepfather, Phil.

"Rebecca, that's a great idea!" Alan exclaimed as he smiled at Mom. "In fact, I was going to suggest the very same thing!" He turned to me. "Lucy, what would you like to order?"

"General Tso's Szechuan Beef," I replied. Out of everything on the menu (we had been coming here forever) it was my absolute favorite.

"Oh, I can't eat that," Laurel said. "It's too spicy for me."

"Laurel has a nervous stomach," Alan explained.

"Dad!" she said, turning red.

It made me feel a little better knowing that major stars also had embarrassing parents. In fact, I kind of felt a little bad for her. "Okay. Then . . . um . . . Sweet and Sour Chicken?" I suggested. "That's not spicy at all. Just sticky. And it's really good here. A lot better than Panda Express in the mall."

She shook her head. "I don't eat chicken."

"Because of your stomach?" I asked.

"No. I just don't like it," she said all matter-of-factly.

The feeling-bad-for-her thing stopped. It would have been one thing if she had seemed a tiny bit sorry about the fact that she kept saying no to all my choices, but she didn't. She didn't even give the teensiest I'm-sorry smile. Instead, it was more like a because-I'm-Laurel-Moses-I-get-my-way-all-the-time smirk.

"Well, what do you want, then?" I asked. "Steamed vegetables and tofu?" That's what Sarah always got, both at Madame Wu's and practically everywhere else. I hated tofu. The one time I had it I spit it out because it tasted like cardboard.

"That sounds great," she replied.

It wasn't like I was serious about it. It was more like I was being sarcastic.

"Well, that was easy!" Mom said. "How about if we get the tofu, and some lo mein—Laurel, that should be okay on your stomach—and, Alan and Laurel, if you like shrimp, we could get some shrimp and lobster sauce . . . that's very mild—"

I hated shrimp!

"And some vegetable dumplings—those aren't spicy at all—" Mom went on.

I liked pork dumplings!

"And some rice," she continued. She turned to them. "Is there anything else you guys would like?"

They shook their heads. "No, that sounds perfect," Alan said. I waited for the "Lucy, is there anything else you'd like?" but it never came. He turned to Laurel. "Doesn't Rebecca have great taste in food?" he said all excitedly. "Every time we go out to eat she always orders the best dishes."

I looked at Mom. Every time? Exactly how many times had there been? She was going to have a lot of explaining to do when we got in the car.

Alan looked at Mom and beamed. "She has great taste in everything."

I had a feeling it was going to be a very long dinner.

Before the food even arrived I had figured out that Laurel was what I called a "parent kid." They're the ones who, when around kids their own age, can barely be bothered to talk to them, but when they're around adults, they don't stop talking. Even though Dad's always telling me that those kids are just as insecure as everyone else, they always make me feel bad about myself, like I'm not as smart or mature as them.

It's not like I didn't try to talk to Laurel, because I did. At least, I tried in between people coming up to her to ask her for autographs. I've never gone up to a famous person to ask for an autograph because other than that time I saw Pirate Petey, the host of the children's show on the local cable access station, in the 7-Eleven, I've never seen one in person. I didn't go up to him because he was too busy screaming at the guy behind the counter that he didn't want 7UP, he wanted Diet 7UP. But if I did go up to one, you can bet that if I accidentally knocked over the soda of the person sitting next to the famous person, I'd at least apologize to the nonfamous person. Especially since the soda stained her T-shirt.

After the people were done asking for autographs (and ruining my clothes), I pretended in my mind that I was a television interviewer and asked Laurel questions like. "Do you miss going to regular school?" and "Do you have any hobbies other than acting and singing?" but it was like she could barely be bothered to answer them. She was an actress, so you'd think that she would at least pretend to want to talk to me. But all I got was short answers like "No, not really" and "Well, I like to read." Later, during the car ride home when I was complaining about it to Mom, she said it was because Laurel was just shy and she was as nervous and uncomfortable as I was, but I didn't buy it. A huge Hollywood star who had stood in front of thousands of people at the MTV Music Awards was shy? I don't think so.

As for me, I'm one of those people who tend to talk a lot when they're nervous or uncomfortable, especially if the other person isn't talking.

I turned to her. "I guess what they say is true," I said,

after I shoveled some more lo mein into my mouth. Mom and Alan were busy playing the "Oh my God—I had no idea you like fill-in-the-blank, too!" game. I was also one of those people who eat a lot when they're nervous.

She dabbed her mouth with her napkin. I didn't even know where mine was. I think it was on the floor. "What's true?" she said.

"That the camera adds ten pounds. Because you're a lot skinnier in person than you are on TV." I meant it as a compliment, but from the look on her face, she wasn't taking it as one. That made me more nervous, which is why I added, "Even though you eat a lot." That didn't make her look any happier.

We went back to not talking for a while. Until she motioned to my cheek and said, "You've got something on your face."

I swiped at it. My coordination problems weren't just with dancing or sports—they were also with food.

"No. Near your nose. A little bit more to the right," she said.

Just then the flash of a camera went off. After my sight finally came back, and Mr. Wu, the owner, had chased the photographer out of the restaurant, Alan explained that the guy had been a "pap." Apparently "pap" was short for "paparazzi," which was Italian for "annoying photographers who take pictures of celebrities when they're trying to do normal things like eat dinner."

"It's still there," Laurel said after Mom and Alan

had gone back to talking about more stuff they had in common. I sat there with my hand clamped on my face and realized what Laurel saw on my face.

"I know. It's just…a pimple," I mumbled from behind my hand.

"A what?"

Of course Laurel Moses didn't recognize the word *pimple*—she had probably never even had one before. "It's a pimple, okay?" I announced loudly, glaring at her.

"Oh," she replied. She could've looked a little sorry about having embarrassed me, but she didn't. "Well, do you have any Preparation H?"

My eyes widened. "Of course not!" I cried. I wasn't exactly sure what Preparation H did, but I had seen the commercials on TV, and I knew it had something to do with problems with your butt.

She shrugged. "That's too bad because just a dab of it totally shrinks pimples," she explained. "My makeup artist uses it on me all the time."

"Thanks, but no thanks," I said. Butt cream on a pimple? Yeah, right.

I looked over at Mom, who was still yammering away to Alan, and beamed her a silent Can-we-please-leave-right-this-very-minute? message. Finally, they stopped talking and turned to us.

"So are you girls having fun?" Mom asked with a big smile.

Couldn't my mother see that I was having one of the

worst nights of my life? Usually, she was one of those parents who liked to talk about feelings all the time ("How did you feel when your two BFFs dumped you, Lucy?" Um, HORRIBLY AND INCREDIBLY AWFUL?), but ever since this whole Alan thing, not only did she not care how I felt, she barely knew I existed.

Both Laurel and I shrugged. At least we agreed on something.

"I was thinking that we'd go back to our house for dessert," Mom said. "Laurel, your dad told me that you love strawberry-rhubarb pie, so I got one of those at the farmers market this afternoon."

My eyes narrowed. I didn't know what I was more upset about: the fact that suddenly it was all about Laurel, or that there was a pie in the house that I hadn't known about. What other secrets was Mom hiding from me? "But what about me? I'm allergic to rhubarb," I said.

Mom turned to me. "Lucy, we've been over this—you're not allergic to rhubarb. You just don't like it."

I was also allergic to beets, liver, anchovies, and sardines. Maybe I didn't have a physical allergy to them where my throat closed up, but wanting to throw up because something tastes so disgusting is a kind of allergy as far as I was concerned.

"So because of that, I also got a French apple one, which you do like," Mom said.

There were two pies in the house? I wasn't allowed

to lock my bedroom door at any time, but my mother could lie to me as much as she wanted?

Alan smiled. "You don't know how happy it makes me that the evening is going as smoothly as it is. I had no idea you girls were going to get along so well!"

If they had been paying attention to us, they would've realized that, actually, we weren't. And unfortunately, it wasn't over yet.

If dinner was "smooth," then dessert was as bumpy as the time we had flown to Florida to go to Disney World and I got so nauseous from the turbulence that I threw up in the throw-up bag they keep in the seat pockets in front of you. The pie helped a little, especially since everyone else went for the strawberry rhubarb, leaving the French apple to me. Well, to me and Miss Piggy, our ten-year-old, eighteen-pound tabby cat who had the bad habit of jumping up on the table when we were eating and just sticking her face in people's dishes. Having grown up with it, I was used to it and didn't find it all that gross, but from the look on Laurel and Alan's faces, they sure did. It wasn't like it was their pie she was trying to eat, just mine, because she doesn't like rhubarb either. Luckily, I was pretty much finished already by the time she got there.

"Miss Piggy, get down!" Mom ordered. She turned to me. "Lucy, why don't you take Laurel upstairs and show her your room while Alan and I finish our coffee? I'm sure she'd enjoy seeing your hat collection."

"Why? So she can throw them in puddles and ruin them all?" is what I wanted to say. But, instead, what I did say was, "Okay."

The floorboards were particularly creaky that night as we walked through the family room. Because our house was built in 1897, everything either creaks or doesn't shut right, like the windows, which makes it super-cold in the winter. Mom likes to say that all that stuff gives the house "character." If you ask me, *character*'s just another word for "old" or "broken." I bet everything in the apartment in New York City where Laurel lived was brand-new.

As we walked up the stairs I thought about how glad I was that Mom had made me clean my room that day because it would have been really embarrassing if Laurel had walked into my room and there had been a pair of underwear in the middle of the floor or something.

Except that when we walked in, there was a pair of underwear in the middle of the floor. "Whoops," I said, lunging for it and throwing it under my bed, which was basically where everything went when Mom told me to clean my room. Thankfully, my closet door was closed (sometimes hard to do when, as part of "cleaning," you throw the stuff that won't fit under the bed in there), so she couldn't see my collection of maxi- and minipads.

Laurel looked around. "I like your room," she finally said. "It's very…colorful."

I couldn't tell if she was lying or not. About whether she liked it; the colorful part was definitely true. The walls were purple (naturally), and I had covered them with all kinds of cool stuff: a colorful tapestry that I had gotten at a Tibetan store in town; some of Dad's photographs; a poster of a famous painting by Picasso that I discovered when I did an oral report on him in fourth grade. I used to have pictures of Rachel and Missy and me up there, too (one had been in a Best Friends Forever frame they had gotten me for my tenth birthday), but obviously I took them down after the dumping. Marissa kept begging me to put up the picture of the two of us that she made her sister take one afternoon that I was over her house in the frame. There was no way I was doing that because (a) we were NOT BFFs and (b) her sister had taken the picture right before I was about to sneeze, so my eyes were closed and my mouth was open.

"Is it true that your closet is the size of this room?" I blurted. Blurting was also something I tended to do when I was nervous. Marissa had told me she read in a magazine that Laurel's closet in New York was the size of most people's bedrooms.

She rolled her eyes. "No. That's just one of the lies they make up about me. Like the one that was in the *National Enquirer* last week about how I'm really an alien. They used this horrible picture where I look bug-eyed."

"What about Jackson Barber? Are you really going out with him?"

She shook her head. "No. I only met him once, in the green room of the Kidz Choice Awards." She walked over to where my hats were hanging on the wall. "You do have a lot of hats, don't you?"

"I actually had one more, but when you threw it in the puddle, it got ruined."

She turned me, and looked confused. "Huh?"

"My red-and-black one?" I reminded her. "The one you thought had lice in it, so you ripped it off your head and threw it on the ground?"

"Ohhh…right. I remember that day. That was you?"

I nodded. I waited for the Oh-my-God-I'm-so-sorry-for-ruining-your-life-how-can-I-ever-make-it-up-to-you part, but I got nothing.

"Sorry about that," was what she said instead, in the same tone as if she had stepped on my toe. "I have a small issue with germs. If you'd like, I can give you some money to replace it."

I almost said, "All the money in the world couldn't make up for how embarrassed I was," but I didn't. Instead, I said, "It wouldn't matter because I already checked and H&M doesn't have any more."

She walked over to my rocking chair and, after brushing off what I guess she thought were germs, sat down. "Come here, Miss Piggy," she called to my cat, who was in the corner trying to clean herself, but because she was so fat she just kept rolling over on her side.

"She won't come," I replied. "She doesn't like

strangers." She didn't really like me, either, even though I was the one who fed her and gave her Greenies cat treats, but I left that part out.

But Miss Piggy struggled to her feet and not only waddled over to Laurel but managed to jump in her lap. Then when Laurel petted her, Miss Piggy started purring.

I was thinking about how unfair it was that everyone in the world thought that Laurel Moses was so great—even cats—when I noticed Miss Piggy's stomach began to move back and forth.

Uh-oh. This was not good.

"Miss Piggy—no!" I yelped. Having lived with her almost my entire life, I knew exactly what was coming. I lunged to pull her off Laurel, but I was too late.

Because right at that moment my cat gagged and threw up a giant hairball on the biggest teen star in the world's lap.

You'd think that with the night ending with a hairball being upchucked, both my mother and Laurel's father would realize that was a pretty strong sign that they should just forget the whole thing and stop seeing each other, but unfortunately, it didn't work out that way. Instead, on Sunday night, after I got home from playing Monopoly with Dad and Sarah, Mom told me that the four of us were going out again the following Friday night. Not only that, but this time it was going to be what she called an "activity outing."

"What?! But why?" I demanded, polishing off the last piece of the French apple pie. It may have been because she felt guilty about dating Alan and all the lying she had been doing, but Mom didn't say anything about the pie, even though, technically, it wasn't exactly the weekend anymore.

"What do you mean why?" she asked. "Because last night went so well."

I waited for her to say something like "I'm just kidding," but she didn't. "Um, it did?" I asked.

From the look on her face, that was not the right thing to say. For the second time that day, I had to sit there and listen to her say how disappointed she was in my behavior. That I hadn't given Laurel a chance, and that she and Dad had raised me to be compassionate and not to judge people, and that, if I had taken the time to have a conversation with Laurel, I would have discovered that not only was she smart and funny and nice, but that leading the life she did—not going to school on a regular basis, acting in a weekly television show, having to travel around the world for movie premieres and award shows—was a very difficult way to grow up.

No school and getting to eat all the free food you wanted in places like Paris doesn't sound all that difficult to me. I almost said it out loud, but I could tell from the way Mom was standing with her hands on her hips and how the little crease between her eyebrows had appeared that it wouldn't go over well. What I did say was, "I'm sorry, but none of my friends would ever embarrass me by pointing out a pimple on my face in the middle of a restaurant." (Even though Marissa probably would have, but technically we weren't friends.)

Even though there was still a good bite and a half on my pie plate, Mom picked it up and walked toward the garbage. "We're going on an activity outing with them next Friday night, and that's that. End of discussion," she said.

At that moment my entire future flashed before my eyes, and it wasn't pretty. Laurel would become my stepsister, and I'd have to spend all my time doing "activities" with her, ones that she was better at than me, while Mom ignored me and yakked away with Alan about all the things they had in common.

If Dr. Maude didn't e-mail me back soon, I was in big trouble.

chapter 5

Dear Dr. Maude,

In case you were wondering, my dinner with Laurel Moses last night was just awful. Not only that, but I just found out that we're going out with them AGAIN. On an "activity outing." So we can "bond." Marissa says it's a very bad sign.

Dr. Maude, what do I do if Laurel ends up becoming my stepsister? Because even though Mom says I haven't given her a chance and she's actually really nice, I like to think I'm a very good judge of character (I'm pretty sure I'm a little psychic), and I don't think she IS very nice, even though she pretends to be when she signs autographs. It wouldn't be all that bad to have a stepbrother or stepsister, but if I did have one, I would want it to be someone normal—not the most popular girl in the world.

I know you're busy, but I really, really, REALLY need some advice about how I can stop my mother from dating Laurel's father and have things go back to the way they were before she came to town to shoot her movie. Otherwise, my life is going to be even more ruined than it has been since sixth grade, and that would NOT be good.

Looking forward to hearing from you.

yours truly,
Lucy B. Parker

"So the *P* in your name isn't for Parker, it's for Picker," huh?" David Murray said as I sat down in my seat a few mornings later as Mrs. Kline boomed, "Take your seats and settle down, people! I said SETTLE DOWN!" over and over. Mrs. Kline had a voice like a foghorn. I had never heard one in real life, but I had heard them on cartoons and, seriously, it sounded just like that.

"What are you talking about?" I asked. Marissa said that Julie Drucker told her that Mark McInerney said at one point that David had a crush on me, but I didn't believe it because (a) Marissa was always lying and (b) he was just such a jerk to me all the time. Dad said that the fact that he was a jerk was actually a very good sign that he did like me because that's how boys act when they like a girl until they're adults. I really hoped Mark didn't have a crush on me because he was just plain gross. Especially since Marissa also told me she had heard that he only brushed his teeth at night rather than in the morning, too.

Now, if Bobby Randall had a crush on me, I wouldn't have minded it so much. In fact, I kind of sort of would've liked it, even though, like I said, I was nervous about having a boyfriend because I didn't want to spend more time crying than I already did. But that probably wasn't going to happen because, according to Marissa, he had a crush on Clementine Durfee.

"Because of the way you're picking your nose in that picture," he replied.

"What picture?" I asked, confused.

"Omigod, Lucy!" screamed Marissa, who had not taken her seat or settled down. Instead, she was over at the class computer with Jacob Fuller. "You didn't tell me you were picking your nose at the Chinese restaurant!" she yelled. "Maybe that's why Laurel Moses wasn't very nice to you!"

"What?" I asked, confused.

"There's a picture of it right here on HotGossip.com," she yelled.

I ran over to the monitor. Sure enough, there it was—the picture that the pap took where I was trying to hide my pimple. And unfortunately, it did look like I was picking my nose. I couldn't believe they put that up on the Internet for everyone to see. Weren't they supposed to get your permission before they did that?

"I was not picking my nose!" I cried. "I was—"

Marissa leaned in and squinted. "Whoops—I was wrong. She's not picking her nose!" she announced. "She's touching that big pimple to the side of it, that's all!"

I was beyond embarrassed. Not as much about the fact that everyone thought I had been picking my nose in front of Laurel Moses, but that Rachel and Missy were right there and were giggling about it.

If I were to ever write an advice book (which I was seriously considering doing because I had been through a lot during my twelve years on the planet, such as divorce and friend-dumping and having no hair), one of the things I would put in the book was that wherever you go, make sure you always have some extra-soft, extra-big Kleenex Ultra Soft tissues in your knapsack. Because even though your mother might yell at you that she's not made of money when she catches you putting half the box in your bag, I'm telling you they're a lot more comfortable to wipe your nose and eyes with than that disgusting extra-scratchy toilet paper in the girls' room if you find yourself in there crying, like I was after everyone laughed at the picture.

As I sat in my favorite stall wiping my eyes, I thought about how even when Laurel Moses wasn't in the room, she still managed to ruin my life. I debated staying in there the entire morning and skipping lunch, until I remembered it was Taco Tuesday and tacos were about the only good thing the cafeteria served. But even the thought of a taco couldn't help me feel better. Why did I always have to be the center of attention all the time nowadays? Why couldn't things just go back to the way they were in fifth grade when I was just considered normal and no one paid that much attention to me? Okay, maybe I hadn't been completely normal on account of the fact that I tended to wear a lot of color at once, but other than that, when my name came up, the only response it got was, "Lucy B. Parker? The Keeper of the Periods? Yeah, I know her. She's nice."

I had thought that nothing could be worse than being dumped by your two BFFs, but I was wrong. Having Laurel Moses in your life was way worse. The only good thing I could see coming out of all this was that at some point I'd be so embarrassed because of something she did that it would have to bring on my period.

"Okay, Lucy, time to buck up," I whispered to myself as I honked into a tissue one last time before standing up and walking over to the sink and splashing water on my face.

The good news was that things couldn't get much worse.

Or could they?

I don't know how I feel about God—like whether He's a guy who looks like Santa Claus but not as fat; or whether there isn't an actual God and instead it's more like what Mom and Dad call "Buddha nature," which is the idea that there's this sort of very wise, very unscared voice within us that will always tell us the right thing to do if we turn off our iPods and get really quiet and listen—but I do know that something seemed to hear my "Okay, Universe, if, by the time I get back to class, something equally embarrassing if not more has happened to someone else so everyone's talking about that now and not me, I promise that not only will I clean my room—like really clean my room—but I will also be nice to Marissa and not roll my eyes when she does something incredibly stupid (which will be tough, but I'll do it anyway)." Because when I got back, the entire class was whispering even though Mrs. Kline kept shouting, "I said, 'Zip it, people'!" and Marissa turned around and said in a normal voice, "Omigod, Lucy—you're not going to believe what you missed—as Mrs. Kline was taking attendance, Kim Mulvaney told Ashima Patel that when she was in the office she overheard the secretaries talking about how Frankie Bankuti was in Mrs. Riley's office right that second because she had heard from a very good source that he broke into Ms. DeMarco's office and STOLE THE MOVIE."

The Movie was gone?! If this was true, I was safe for a while because this was big news. Like two-days'-worth-of-gossip news. The real title of the Movie was *What's Happening to Me?* and it was about puberty. Obviously we all already knew about that stuff (since like fourth grade) but according to Malika Connors, a seventh grader on my bus, not only did the Movie talk about what happened to boys, too (meaning e-r-e-c-t-i-o-n-s), but there was a naked woman in it, too. And not just a drawing of one, but a real one. That's why you had to get your parents to sign a permission slip saying it was okay for you to see it—*because it was that shocking*. But then the school did something really jerky, which was that after you brought the slip back, they refused to tell you when they were going to show it in health class, probably so that you'd make sure to come to school instead of pretending to be sick and staying home.

Everyone talked about what might happen to Frankie, and where the Movie might be, and if perhaps a screening could be set up at his house so we could all see it there. By this time Mrs. Kline had given up on us and said, "Fine. Act like savages. See if I care. I'm going to get some coffee." Then an even crazier thing happened. Rachel and Missy got out of their seats and walked up to me and Rachel said, "Hi Lucy," like it was a totally normal thing for her to do. Like she hadn't ignored me for the last four and half months.

"Hi?" I said, nervously, looking around to make sure no one was filming this and I wasn't going to end up on *America's Most Embarrassing Moments*.

"We have a question," Rachel said.

"What is it?" I asked. I hoped my voice sounded natural because I sure didn't feel natural inside.

Rachel looked at Missy, who nodded for her to go on. She turned back to me. "So are you, like, BFFs with

Laurel Moses now?" I was all set to say, "Of course we're not because (a) she's totally stuck up and (b) frankly, I'm not ready to have a new BFF because of what you guys did to me." But what came out was, "Well, I wouldn't say we're best friends, but we're getting to be really good friends."

What?! I had no idea where that had come from. I had just totally and completely lied.

Missy's mouth fell open so wide I could see all her fillings. "Really?" she asked.

Here was my chance to fix things. To say, "Well, no. I just said that because I thought if I did, you might think I was cool and want to be my friend again, but it's actually a big lie. The truth is I can't stand her, and I'm completely dreading having to see her again on Friday when we have to go on an activity outing."

But instead I just said: "Yeah. We're hanging out on Friday night again." I couldn't believe it—I was turning into a massive liar just like Marissa! At least the second half of that was true, even if the "yeah" part wasn't. It took everything in me to not clamp my hand over my mouth to shut myself up. But they looked so impressed, just like they did back in fifth grade when we found out that Elizabeth Milken got her period on May 22 at 3:05 p.m. (the first entry in the purple notebook that said "The Official Period Log of Sixth-Grade Girls at Jefferson Middle School in Northampton, MA"), and that made me feel good.

"Wow. That's so cool," Rachel said. "So, um, listen. It's my birthday in two weeks—"

Um, duh. Her birthday was January 28. And Missy's was on July 17.

"And I'm having a sleepover—" she continued.

Double duh. It's all the girls in the class were talking about. Practically every single one of them had been invited, except Marissa and Cindy Carter and me. Cindy was never invited to anything anymore ever since it got around that even though she came from one of the richest families in town, she was a kleptomaniac who stole from stores and other kids' houses.

"My mom arranged for two women from the nail salon to come over and give us all manicures and pedicures and everything. Anyway, so if you really are good friends with Laurel Moses now, I was thinking that the two of you would like to come."

My hands got clammy again. "You want me to come to your birthday party, and bring Laurel Moses?"

The two of them nodded.

I was stunned. Obviously I wanted to go to the party, but how was I going to get out of this? I couldn't bring Laurel with me. I hated Laurel, and I don't think she liked me very much either.

When Mrs. Kline came back into the room, she started banging on her desk with her gavel. "Okay, enough! SETTLE DOWN NOWWWWW!"

The room suddenly got quiet. Everyone knew that

when Mrs. Kline drew out the "now" in "Settle down now," she meant business. Personally, as much as I hated mixed fractions, which is what we were about to do, I was glad class was about to start, because I needed some quiet to figure out how I was going to get Laurel Moses to come to Rachel's sleepover with me.

Mrs. Kline droned on and on. Marissa kept raising her hand and saying, "Ooh, ooh—I know! I know," but got the answer wrong every time. And I thought about the best way to handle this. By the end of the period I had figured out I had two options: I could lie AGAIN and say that while Laurel would love to come, unfortunately, she was going to be in India visiting needy children and so I'd be more than happy to come by myself. Then I realized that, because Laurel was so famous there were like ten thousand websites that talked about her on a daily basis, including WheresLaurelNow.com, and it would be easy enough for them to find out that, actually, she was still in Northampton and would be until the middle of February. Especially if there were more paparazzi pictures of the two of us together with me looking horrible. Or, I could suck it up and be really nice to Laurel and spend the next two weeks trying to really become friends with her, and then ask her to come. Chances were she wouldn't want to waste her time with plain old regular girls like us, but maybe if I told her the whole story she'd realize that, I, too, was a needy child. Obviously not in a no-shoes-like-kids-in-India kind of way, but in other ways. Like

I-really-wish-I-had-my-old-BFFs-back-because-hanging-out-with-Marissa-is-driving-me-crazy kind of way.

I could only hope that seventh grade would be a little easier.

That is, if I made it till then.

chapter 6

Dear Dr. Maude,

You must be really busy because you haven't written me back yet. I hope that everything's okay and that nothing happened to your dogs, Id and Ego.

Anyway, the reason I'm writing again is because now I have ANOTHER problem in addition to the Laurel Moses stuff. I won't go into all of it now, because it's kind of a long story, but basically what happened was, right before sixth grade started, I got dumped by my two BFFs, Rachel and Missy. And I still really miss them, even if what they did was completely mean and horrible and I myself would never, ever do something so cruel to another human being. But on Monday, Rachel invited me to her birthday sleepover. I know you're probably thinking, So what's the problem? That sounds great, but the problem is that she wants me to bring Laurel, because I kind-of, sort-of told her that Laurel and I had become very good friends. Which, of course, we have not, and the only reason I said it in the first place was to try and impress her so she'd want to be my friend again.

I want you to know that unlike Marissa, I do not lie

a lot. Maybe once in a while, like about whether I've truly cleaned my room or just shoved everything under my bed, but that's about it.

If you could give me advice about what to do, I'd really appreciate it.

yours truly,
Lucy B. Parker

Maybe if Marissa's idea about Friday night had worked, Laurel and I would have become friends. And I could have invited her to Rachel's party. And she would have said yes. And Rachel and Missy would have realized they had made a humongous mistake dumping me. And everything would have gone back to the way it had been, including Laurel going back to New York City and leaving us all alone.

Marissa's idea—which she brought up to me as we sat in the bleachers during gym class on Friday morning (it had been a Please-excuse-Lucy-B.-Parker-from-gym-today-on-account-of-the-fact-that-she-is-menstruating note day), watching Brooke Naylor try to serve the ball in volleyball and fail miserably for the seventh time (she was even more coordination-challenged than I was)—was that the activity we all do on Friday night be bowling.

"Hmm…that's not a bad idea," I replied. I bet Laurel Moses had never been bowling in her life, if only because you had to wear shoes that had been on other people's feet. For someone who had a problem with germs and completely freaked out when another person's hat was on her head (even when that other person DID NOT have lice), wearing used shoes would be hard. She was rich enough to have bought her own shoes, but I just didn't think she was a bowling kind of person. I, on the other hand, was a bowling kind of person. Even though it required coordination, I was pretty good at it. I had a lot of practice because so many kids in Northampton had their birthday parties at Spare Time, the local bowling alley. Some of them had their parties at the roller skating place, Interskate 91 North in Hadley, but I didn't like those parties nearly as much because I was not good at roller skating and spent most of those parties holding on to the railing. Maybe if we went bowling and Laurel saw how good I was, she'd ask me to give her bowling lessons.

"I knew you'd like it!" Marissa exclaimed. "See? That's why we make such great BFFs—because I know you so well! It's like I'm psychic or something!"

I rolled my eyes. If she were psychic, she'd know that we were not BFFs and never would be.

Still, the bowling thing was a good idea, and I sure did need a few of those right about now.

Unfortunately, Mom didn't agree.

"Oh honey, I know how much you like bowling, but

I don't think that's going to work," she said that evening as she looked in the freezer for her keys so we could leave and not be late like we usually were. If a stranger had been there, they would've thought, Why on earth is that woman looking in the freezer for her keys? but if you knew Mom, you'd know that for some reason a lot of things ended up in the freezer. Keys, her reading glasses. Once, when I opened it to grab a Popsicle, I found her purse in there.

"Why not?" I asked, using the oven as a mirror as I tried to fix my red beret so it sat just so on my head, which is very hard to do. I had a lot of berets in my hat collection though because (a) you could fold them up and they wouldn't get ruined and (b) they were only $6.98 at H&M. I had decided to wear it that night—along with jeans, my Wonder Woman T-shirt, and a navy cardigan (so it would be harder for Mom to tell I wasn't wearing my bra)—because it would be easy to bowl in than one of my floppier hats that might screw up my vision as I was about to throw the ball.

Mom, on the other hand, was wearing a very unbowling-like outfit—a black sweater and her favorite flowy pink-and-blue embroidered Indian skirt. Dad and I had gotten her the skirt for her forty-fifth birthday, the last one we had all spent together before they got divorced. Maybe that's why she didn't want to go bowling; she didn't want to change and make us even later.

"Move, Miss Piggy," Mom said as she hoisted the cat

off the counter. Miss Piggy liked to lie next to the pantry most of the time because that's where her food was kept. You didn't get the name Miss Piggy if you didn't love to eat.

As always, when Mom grabbed her, Miss Piggy didn't yowl or hiss or bite her, which is what she did when I touched her.

"Well, I think Alan would be afraid that Laurel would get hurt," Mom said.

"Get hurt bowling?" I asked. I could understand a person getting hurt roller skating, but bowling? If you dropped the ball on your foot, maybe, but from what I had seen on YouTube of Laurel singing and dancing at the Super Bowl, she had no problem with coordination. In fact, like everything else about her, it had been perfect.

After not finding her keys in the pantry, Mom shut the door. "Let's just say he's a little ... neurotic when it comes to her safety."

"You're going out with someone who's neurotic?" I asked, worried. That wasn't good. *Neurotic* had been one of our vocabulary words back in November, so I knew it meant "crazy."

"He's a New Yorker—of course he's neurotic," Mom replied. "He's a little ... overprotective when it comes to Laurel. I'm sure it has to do with Laurel's mom."

Laurel was stuck-up and she had falsely accused me of having lice (which I DID NOT have), but at that moment I put everything aside. I felt really bad for her. Everyone knew the story about Laurel's mom because for some reason reporters liked to ask her about it. If you asked me, it was a really mean thing to do. In fact, in one interview she had done before the Academy Awards last year, Laurel actually started crying because the reporter wouldn't shut up about it.

When Laurel was seven, her mom was diagnosed with cancer. Even though the doctors thought that they could get rid of it and she would be totally fine, that's not what happened. What happened was that the cancer moved to her brain, and she was dead in like a month. And for part of that month, she was in a coma, which meant that Laurel didn't even get a chance to say good-bye to her because when you're in a coma, it's like a very, very deep sleep and you can't hear anything—even something really loud like a garbage truck or a snowplow. The whole thing was so sad that when I watched Laurel talk about it, I started crying, too. Sometimes Mom bugged me (like when I'd say, "Just give me one perfectly good reason why I can't fill-in-the-blank," and she'd say, "Because I'm the mother, that's why. End of discussion."), but I don't know what I'd do if she died. Obviously I'd still have Dad (as long as he didn't get cancer, too). But I think I'd be so sad that I'd almost want to die, too. Even though I wasn't entirely convinced that, when you did die, you went to heaven so you could be with all the people you loved who had gone there before you like your mother, and your grandfather, and any pets you had.

But still, even though I felt bad for Laurel because

of the no-mother thing, it didn't mean I wanted to do an activity with her. "So what are we going to do, then?" I asked.

Not finding her keys underneath the sink, Mom stood up and smiled at me. Was it my imagination, or were her teeth a million times brighter than they usually were? Did she use one of those teeth-whitening kits they show on TV? I made a mental note to ask Marissa if her mom had started whitening her teeth when she started dating Phil. "I thought we'd go do karaoke!" she announced. "Doesn't that sound fun?"

Fun?! When you have such a bad voice that your own chorus teacher asks you to please not sing but instead just mouth the words, the idea of standing up in front of a roomful of people—including the person who had the number one downloaded song on iTunes for the last seven weeks in a row—did not sound fun. It sounded like a punishment.

chapter 7

Dear Dr. Maude,

While Mom's looking for her keys, I decided to check my e-mail to see if you had written back yet. Because now I have ANOTHER problem. Mom just told me we're going to do karaoke with Laurel and her dad. Most people would think that sounds like a lot of fun, but not me. I have a REALLY BAD voice, and Laurel just happens to be one of the greatest singers in history. (Personally, I don't agree, but that's what it says on her website.)

Seriously, I feel like I'm going to throw up. And I'm definitely going to have to wear a pad tonight because Marissa says that her sister told her that extreme nervousness can bring on your period. I know you're a psychologist rather than a medical doctor, but would you happen to know if that's true?

Okay, Mom just yelled up that her keys were hanging on the hook next to the door (which is exactly where they're supposed to be but usually never are, which is why we never look there), so I have to go. If you do write me back, I won't get the e-mail until after the Karaoke

Thing. In fact, if I die of embarrassment, I won't get it at all, but I'd appreciate it if you wrote back, anyway.

yours truly,
Lucy B. Parker

If, for once in her life, Marissa was right and extreme nervousness did bring on your period, I totally would have gotten mine while standing up in front of the crowd that night. But, as usual, she was wrong, and I didn't get it, even though I kept running to the bathroom to check. I even brought a pantiliner to put on top of the pad, just to be safe. You would've thought that finally getting my period was the least that God could've done to make up for all the embarrassment and humiliation I had been through ever since Laurel came into my life, but no.

But before the Karaoke Thing, first we had to go to dinner at Flo's Fishery, one of my least favorite restaurants in all of Hampshire County. Laurel had anemia, which meant that there was something wrong with her blood and she needed to eat a lot of iron, which, Mom told me, was a major ingredient in fish. Later on when I got home I looked it up on the Internet (anemia, not fish), and it said that sometimes you got anemia if your periods were really heavy, which sounded both very scary and kind of interesting. If Laurel and I had actually been friends, I would have asked her if her periods were really heavy and what brand of pads she found to be the best. But because we weren't, that would've been really weird dinner conversation.

"But I hate fish," I whispered to Mom as we stood in the lobby of the Hotel Northampton as Alan called the restaurant to see if we needed a reservation (if he had bothered to ask me, I could've told him that we didn't, on account of the fact that most normal people knew that fish was disgusting and therefore the place was never crowded).

Mom had come up with the dumb idea that we go pick Alan and Laurel up at their hotel, and then all drive over to the restaurant together because it would give us more time for the four of us to bond. The minute she used the B-word, I got nervous because, just the other day, as Marissa was tagging along as I went to get a cupcake after school, she said, "Now your mom hasn't used the B-word yet, has she?" When I asked what the B-word was (baby? boob?), she told me it stood for bonding, which, when used when talking about a parent's new boyfriend/girlfriend and his/her kids meant big trouble. It meant that Things Were Getting Serious, which, according to Marissa, was code for "I'm definitely going to marry this person."

"That's not true, Lucy. You like fried clams," Mom whispered back as she smiled at a rich-looking woman walking through the lobby. The Hotel Northampton was the nicest hotel in town, so it made sense that Laurel was staying there. There was a rumor going around the Internet that Laurel was so rich that when she took baths in a hotel, she filled the tub with bottled water. I found that hard to believe because that was a total waste of water, and everyone knew from all the public service announcements she did on TV that Laurel was very into saving the environment. Plus, if you used bottled water, it wouldn't be hot, so you'd basically be taking a room-temperature bath.

"I only like the fried clams from Friendly's," I replied. I loved Friendly's—not only the Fribbles, which were basically super-thick milk shakes, but they also had excellent fried clams (extra crunchy) and Jumbo Fronions, which were ginormous onion rings. "Clams are fish, so why don't we go to Friendly's and Laurel can just have those."

"Lucy, we're going to Flo's, and that's that. End of discussion," Mom said firmly.

I could not believe how unfair my mother was being. My entire life my friends had always said how cool my mom was and how she always talked to kids like they were people instead of kids. But since this Alan thing had started? Forget it. She had used the phrase "That's that. End of discussion" more in the last week than she had my entire life.

I was all set to tell Mom all of that and then some—including the fact that making people wait for so long (we had been waiting for Laurel for ten minutes, after Alan had said, "Laurel's on the phone with her agent and will be down in two minutes") was very rude—when the elevator door opened and everyone in the lobby started buzzing. It was just like that day on the movie set.

"Sorry I'm late," Laurel said as she walked toward us wearing a very non-bowling-appropriate outfit (a really cool patchwork-looking dress and cowboy boots) and the fake movie-star smile that she always smiled when she was interviewed on the red carpet before a fancy premiere. "My agent and I were talking about this movie they offered me that shoots in Africa."

"You get to go to Africa?!" I blurted. I was so amazed I forgot we weren't really friends and therefore I was supposed to be more polite, and quiet, especially because we were in a public place. As far as I was concerned, traveling around the world sounded like the number one best thing about being a huge star. And Africa was the place I wanted to visit most in the world, on account of the fact that *Mutual of Omaha's Wild Kingdom* was one of my favorite television shows and a lot of it took place there. In fact, when I grew up, I thought maybe I could work for the Jane Goodall Institute, which was where they studied primates like chimps and apes.

I don't think Laurel was used to people yelling around her because she looked a little freaked out. Which was too bad. We would definitely never be friends because I tend to yell a lot, and my voice is on the loud side even when I'm not yelling. "Well, yeah, but I had to say no."

Why would anyone not want to go to Africa? "Because of your TV show?" I asked.

She shook her head. "No. Because of malaria."

"What?" I asked.

"It's a disease you get from getting bitten by mosquitoes," she explained.

"Wait a minute—you're giving up a trip to Africa because you might get bitten by a bug?" I asked.

"Between one and three million people die from it a year," she said defensively. "Mostly in Africa. So, yes, I'm giving up a trip to Africa," she said before she turned on her cowboy boot heel and marched toward the exit.

Yeah, this was never going to work.

All through dinner Alan tried his best to get Laurel and me to bond by pointing out things we had in common. "Look at that—you both like lemon in your water!" he exclaimed. "Amazing—both of you only eat the middle of the bread, but not the crust!" he marveled. "What are the odds that neither of you like onions?!" he gasped. Actually, I did like onions—I just didn't want to risk having bad breath so Laurel could have one more reason to think I was just a dumb, unsophisticated twelve-year-old while she was a huge fourteen-year-old star. I knew that's what she thought of me, because when I tried to be nice, so the sleepover thing could actually work out, I said, "I really like your dress." She said "Thanks" in sort of a shy way that almost made me like her a little. It always made me feel better to find out that other people are shy like I was, even though I was loud sometimes. But then she ruined the whole thing when, after staring at my outfit, she said "I like your T-shirt. I was just reading about how it's very hip now to dress retro." No one had ever called me hip before, and that part was pretty cool, but everyone knew that being called retro—which meant old-fashioned—was an insult.

Thankfully, before Alan could get back to his let's-talk-about-what-else-Lucy-and-Laurel-have-in-common (um, how about "Wow—you're both girls!"?), Mom interrupted. "Laurel, I was thinking that, after dinner, in an attempt for all of us to bond even more, we could go karaokeing!"

Laurel's face, which was normally all tan and healthy looking, turned pretty white. "Bond?" she said nervously. For a minute there, I wondered if she had a friend whose mother had remarried and had told her about the B-word and Things Getting Serious and all that other stuff. Marissa's "The Unofficial Guide to Everything Laurel Moses" said that Sequoia, the girl who played her BFF on the show, was also her BFF in real life, too. And Sequoia was the only kid her age I had seen in any of the pictures on the gazillion blogs that followed every single thing Laurel did. All the other pictures had Laurel with that hair guy and that makeup woman I'd seen at the Hat Incident, or with a woman in her twenties whose face was all orange like she had eaten too many carrots (that's what happened to Dalia, a babysitter I had when I was five), who the sites said was Jaycee, her personal assistant. If Laurel and I had been friends, I would have asked her what it was like to order around someone who was ten years older than you, because I bet it was really cool, but since we weren't, I didn't.

Mom nodded. "You, more than anyone, know that music is such a wonderful way to express yourself and your feelings."

Oh no. If Mom started getting all let's-talk-about-feelings-and-have-a-giant-group-hug, I was going to kill her. That was a very Northampton thing to do. And it was a very Mom thing to do. It drove me nuts, not to mention it was totally embarrassing.

"I can't believe I'm admitting this," Mom said, "but the other day when your song 'Millions of Miles' came on the radio, I got so choked up I had to pull over to the side of the road."

Oh brother.

Alan grabbed for her hand. "Oh honey, you didn't tell me that!" Wait a minute—were his eyes getting all shiny like he was going to cry? "I'm so moved that you were so moved," he said, all emotional.

Oh double brother.

Mom nodded. "I know I'm a grown woman, but the song just really took me back to my own youth and what it was like to experience my first big crush."

I knew that song. Everyone knew that song. It was about a girl who's unpopular and one day she locks eyes with the most popular boy in the grade across the cafeteria, even though he sits a million miles away from her (that's where the title comes from) and it's like instant true love, but they can't be together because he's dating the most popular girl in school. The whole thing is very sad, and you really believe Laurel when she sings, "I'm just a lonely girl looking to be just a little less lonely with you." Though (a) I found it hard to believe Laurel was lonely, and (b) any boy would dump his girlfriend to go out with her. I did wonder, though, if Laurel had a crush on anyone and exactly how much like Madison— the boy-crazy character she played on the show—she really was. If we were friends, I would've asked her, but we weren't, so I didn't.

"Thanks," Laurel said. "But I don't think I should sing tonight." She cleared her throat and coughed. "I think I'm, uh, coming down with something."

Alan reached out and started feeling her forehead and cheek. "You didn't mention that," he said nervously. "What's wrong? Is it your throat? Your stomach? Do you have a headache?"

"It's, um, just an all-over kind of thing," she said, not looking at him. "But I'll be fine. I mean, as long as I don't sing."

There were three reasons I could tell she was totally lying about being sick: (1) even though she was an award-winning actress, that was one of the fakest-sounding coughs I had ever heard; (2) she didn't look him in the eye when she said it was an all-over thing; and

(3) everyone knew that when you were lying, you tended to use "uh" and "um" a lot.

"I think we should get you home then," Alan said anxiously. "You have some really big scenes to shoot on Monday and—"

"No, no!" she said. "I want to go. I'll just watch you guys do it. It'll be fun." She looked at me and smiled. (Later on in the car after we dropped them off, Mom insisted that it had not been an evil smile, that it was a perfectly genuine smile, and that if I didn't stop with this Laurel-Moses-has-it-out-for-me stuff, she didn't know what she was going to do with me. That made me shut up for a while because "I don't know what I'm going to do with you" was almost as bad as "or else" and "end of story.")

Having to sing in front of Laurel Moses like she was a judge on *American Idol* would be fun? I would have rather gotten my appendix out. And been fully awake for it.

Everyone knows that when adults do karaoke, they're going to look stupid. It's just one of the things you can count on like, say, rain when you're supposed to go on a field trip to Boston and walk the Freedom Trail. If you ask me, I think it's because something about the whole thing makes them go back to being whatever kind of person they were like when they were teenagers, before they grew up and got all serious because of all the bills they had to pay.

For instance, when Mom got up in front of everyone at Bishop's Lounge and sang an old Madonna song called "Lucky Star," she started acting all sexy, swiveling her hips and shaking her hair. That made sense because Mom was really wild when she was teenager and used to sneak out of her bedroom after she was supposed to be asleep and drive to the beach with her boyfriend and make out in the car. I knew this not because she told me, but because I heard her and my grandmother talking about it once when I was overlistening from the top of the stairs. I had always thought it was kind of cool that Mom had been a little crazy back then. But what was not cool was that she was acting like this in front of a huge room full of strangers.

As for Alan, when he got up there and sang some dorky song I had never heard of called "Heartlight" by some guy I had never heard of called Neil Diamond, and his eyes got all shiny and he got all emotional about it, I could tell that back in high school, he had probably been just as dorky and just as much a nerd as he was now. I personally don't mind nerds—in fact, I find them to be really nice, most likely because they don't want anyone to have to feel like they feel when people pick on them. Like Mom, he really got into the song, which, even though I wasn't related to him, I found embarrassing.

At least Laurel and I agreed on one thing—that Alan looked like an idiot—because when I looked over at her, she had slunk down so far in her seat you could basically see only her head. I felt pretty bad for her because by that time, people had figured out that the blonde girl who looked like Laurel Moses actually was Laurel Moses, so they were staring more at her than at Alan. At least there were only like ten other people there, but still.

People must have started texting their friends that Laurel was there because by the time a few more people had gotten through their songs (one lady who looked sort of like a lunchroom aide sang a Britney Spears song, and her husband sang a song by this guy Jimi Hendrix, complete with air guitar), Bishop's Lounge was packed. Like maybe fifty or sixty people. "I can't believe I'm going to get to hear Laurel Moses sing live!" I heard one woman say to another as I went to the bathroom. Then, as I walked back to the table, I heard a guy say to his friend, "Dude, I am so filming this on my iPhone and putting this on YouTube."

"You know, everyone thinks you're going to sing," I said to Laurel after I managed to fight my way through the crowd back to my seat.

"Well, I'm not," she said stubbornly.

Jeez. It was hard to keep feeling bad for someone when she kept being a jerk to you even when you were just trying to make conversation and find a way to maybe become friends. "How come?" I asked.

She turned to me. "You really want to know why?"

I nodded.

"Because I can tell that you already don't like me, and if I get up there and sing, you'll probably find a reason to like me even less, and I'm just not in the mood for that to happen," she said. "Especially now that they're using words like *bonding,* which means that this whole thing might be getting serious and we might end up being stepsisters."

"You think that's going to happen?" I asked nervously.

She shrugged. "If they keep that stuff up, it probably will," she said, motioning to Mom and Alan, who were sitting close together. I don't know what it was he was whispering to her, but it sure was making her giggle.

I had to say her not singing was pretty nice of her. I mean, if I had an amazing voice, I'd sing all the time— especially in public.

"I don't not like you," I blurted out.

That stuck-up look on her face that seemed to be a permanent fixture unless she plastered on the fake movie-star smile disappeared, and Laurel looked like a regular fourteen-year-old girl. A super-pretty one, but still, she looked more normal than I had ever seen her. "Really?" she said.

I shrugged. Even though she insulted my clothes and was giving up a trip to Africa, I guess she wasn't that bad. She was definitely a lot better than Marissa. That being said, if she ended up coming to the sleepover with me, and Rachel and Missy decided they wanted to be BFFs with her instead of me, I'd never talk to her again.

Just then three women came over the table. "Are you going to sing?" one of them demanded.

Laurel put her movie-star smile back on. "No, sorry—

I'm not," she said sweetly. "But I'd be happy to sign an autograph for you."

"But we want to hear you sing," one of the other women said. She held up her BlackBerry. "I have the camera all set up and everything."

"Thanks, but I'm not really prepared," Laurel said. It was pretty amazing how, when there was a crowd around, she always managed to completely keep her cool. If it were me, I would've said, "Obviously you got an F in Manners because that's just plain rude!"

The woman turned. "Hey, she says she won't sing!" she called out to the crowd.

From the way everyone started grumbling, you would've thought it was Free Scoop Saturday at Scoops and they had just announced they had run out of ice cream. In fact, the crowd got so upset that Laurel got all nervous and grabbed my arm. "But my friend here—"

I couldn't believe it—Laurel Moses had called me her friend! That meant if I asked her to Rachel's sleepover, she'd totally say yes!

"—she'll sing," she said.

"What?!" I whispered. Was Laurel completely insane? Friends don't make friends who are tone-deaf get up in front of a ginormous crowd and sing. "No, I won't!"

"Why not?"

"Because I'm a horrible singer!" I replied.

"Oh, come on. I bet you're not," she whispered back. "Everyone says that, but no one's that bad."

I gave her a look. "Oh, I am. Trust me."

"Lucy, I think it's a great idea for you go up there and express yourself," Mom chimed in.

"If I could go up there and embarrass myself, anyone can," said Alan. I shot him a look. "Not that you're going to embarrass yourself," he quickly added.

"If the girl in the hat sings, will you sing afterward?" someone in the crowd called out to Laurel.

"Ah...maybe," she sputtered.

"Get up there and sing, then!" someone else yelled.

I was wrong. The Hat Incident was not the most embarrassing moment of my life. Having a picture of me not picking my nose splashed all over the Internet was not the most embarrassing moment of my life either. This was the most embarrassing moment of my life. I could've run out the door and escaped. But then I'd be forever known as The Girl with the Hat Who Was Too Scared to Get Onstage and Do Karaoke. And who wanted to be known as that girl?

"It won't be so bad. I promise," Laurel whispered as I took a deep breath and stood up.

Ha. Famous last words.

As I made my way up to the microphone, all I could think of was if I didn't get my period after this, life was completely unfair.

I looked at the list of songs to choose from; of course there were like five Laurel Moses songs. There were also a bunch of Britney ones, some Katy Perrys, some Taylor Swifts, and a whole lot of Beyoncé that I knew, but the last thing I was going to do was stand up in front of a huge crowd of people and shake my butt. Sure, I did that alone in my bedroom with the door closed tight and a chair shoved up against it so Mom couldn't come in, but not here. Finally, after what seemed like forever, I ended up choosing "Let It Be" by the Beatles. I knew the song by heart because of our fourth-grade chorus recital, even if I had only been allowed to mouth it. Plus, no one expected you to shake your butt to that song.

I walked up to the stage and took the mic. Everyone was looking at me. After some major throat clearing, I began.

"When I find myself in times of trouble," I sang. Except then I had to stop because the microphone did that feedback thingy where it made a screeching noise and everyone in the crowd covered their ears and a look came over their face like they had just swallowed a mixture of peanut butter and lox. "Uh, sorry," I said. I turned to the guy who was in charge of the karaoke machine. "Can I start again?"

He rolled his eyes and started it from the beginning.

"When I find myself in times of trouble," I sang again. There was no feedback this time, but the crowd had a nauseated look on their faces. And by the time I got to the "Let it be, let it be / Let it be, let it be" chorus part, they looked even more nauseous, even though I tried to put what Ms. Edut, my chorus teacher, called "some real soul" into it. From Laurel's expression, I could tell she wished she could take back her "No one's that bad." Even my own mother looked scared—like she was afraid that if I didn't stop soon, I might burst someone's eardrum. Not only was I a really bad singer, but I was a really loud singer to boot, and here I had a microphone.

I was so nervous, and I was sweating so much, and I was so nervous that the people in the audience could see how much I was sweating, that when I got to the third verse I just blanked out and completely forgot it. Even though I totally knew it by heart because Ms. Edut had made us practice it three billion times because she always wants everything to be perfect. Sure, the words were right there on the machine in front of me, but because I was so nervous, I had gone temporarily blind. So instead of singing, I just stood there in front of the ginormous crowd, sweating but not singing, and completely sure that I had just gotten my period.

Finally, Mom yelled out, "It's okay, honey. You can do it. Just keep going." And then when I didn't, she started singing with—or, rather, for—me at the "Mother Mary comes to me" part. Which made me totally cringe because, like I said, her voice wasn't all that much better than mine. And also, the last thing I needed was my mom to come to my rescue in front of everyone. Finally, the karaoke guy let the music fade out, and I was done.

Needless to say, not a lot of people clapped when

I was done. Only three—Mom, Alan, and Laurel. Not only were they clapping, but they were clapping really loud and yelling, "Yeah, Lucy! That was great!" like they were at a concert for their favorite singer in the world. The rest of the crowd just looked really confused, and still a little nauseated, like they weren't quite sure what had just happened. At least they didn't boo, because that would've been really awful.

"Hey, Laurel, now will you get up and sing?" someone yelled after I slunk back to my seat.

"I—um—" she sputtered.

"Yeah! You promised!" yelled someone else.

I was about to yell out that she hadn't promised, but I didn't think anyone was interested in hearing anything more from me.

The whole room started buzzing, and the louder it got, the more you could tell they were getting mad—like if Laurel didn't go up there right that second, there might be a giant stampede and we'd all be crushed to death.

"Honey, maybe you should give them one song," Alan said.

"But—"

I felt like saying, "Yeah, go on up there, because there's no way I could like you less than I do right now," but I didn't. Instead, I just gave her a dirty look before I crossed my arms and turned away from her.

"If you don't, it's going to be all over the blogs and it could really hurt your image," he said.

She sighed. "Fine," she said as she stood up. It was the same "Fine" I had used earlier in the evening when Mom had told me to get back in the house right that minute and put my bra on before we went to pick up Laurel and Alan. Laurel even stomped up to the stage like I had.

"Sing 'Broken Promises'!"

"No—'Millions of Miles'!"

It must be hard when you're a famous person doing karaoke because no matter what song you choose, everyone knows it's you the famous person singing it rather than someone unfamous like me. In the end Laurel ended up choosing the song "Beautiful" by Christina Aguilera, which happened to be one of my favorite songs. At first when she started to sing it, she seemed a little awkward and shy—at one point during the first verse, she even screwed up a few notes—but as it went on, she got more comfortable and her voice got stronger. She got so into it that when I looked around, all these people were crying—including Mom and even some of the guys.

The fact that a few times that night I had felt bad for her and thought maybe she wasn't so bad and we could become friends? Well, after she was done and everyone in the room stood up and gave her a standing ovation and she bowed a bunch of times and said, "Thank you! Thank you very much! Oh, you guys are just the best!" with a huge smile on her face, it wiped that possibility right out. A friend didn't (a) force someone with a horrible singing voice to go onstage only to then (b) go up there after her and completely show her up like that.

She took more bows and blew kisses to the audience, and I saw Mom and Alan clapping wildly for her. "Isn't she just great?" Mom said proudly to the woman next to her, as if Laurel was her own daughter. What if that happened? What if all this bonding really did result in Things Getting Serious and they got married and we became stepsisters? I could see it now— everything I did, Laurel would do a bajillion times better. I'd get an A, and Laurel would get an A . I'd get a boyfriend, and Laurel would get a cuter boyfriend. I'd make red velvet cupcakes and Laurel would make a three-layer red velvet cake with little silver balls decorating the top of it.

I looked over at Mom and Alan, and they were kissing. In front of everyone. Like they were a couple who were thisclose to getting engaged and getting married.

This was not good. In fact, this was very, very bad.

There was no way I was spending the rest of my life known as Laurel Moses's Untalented Stepsister.

chapter 8

Dear Dr. Maude,

Even though you still haven't written me back, I thought I'd try again, just in case my other e-mails went to your spam folder or something like that. So if this is the first e-mail you're getting from me, please check the folder because there's probably a bunch in there.

I know from watching your show that most of the time, you try to help people get to a place where they CAN get married, but the reason I'm writing today is because I was wondering if you could give me some advice as to what a person might do if they're trying to get people to NOT get married. Because if those two people DID get married, then I'd have the worst stepsister in the entire world. If you've read my other e-mails, you know that I'm talking about Laurel Moses. I won't go into all of it now, because it's kind of a long story, but I can promise you that after what happened the other night at karaoke, you would totally agree that having Laurel as a stepsister would ruin my entire life.

It's not like my mom is officially engaged (YET), but this morning she told me that she and Alan are going to New York City for the weekend. Marissa says that means she'll be coming back with a ring on her finger. She said one night away is okay (so they can have some privacy to really "do it"—ew!), but that two nights when you're not married is serious. That's what happened when her mom and Phil went to Atlantic City for a weekend. He proposed to her in front of the slot machines and then he took her for the all-you-can-eat steak-and-lobster dinner.

Would you happen to know if this is true? Because if it is, I'm REALLY going to have to try to stop them. Oh, and when my mother was packing, I saw that she put in her lacy black underwear AND a red silk nightgown, which I'm thinking can't be a good sign either.

Thanks in advance.

yours truly,
Lucy B. Parker

On Monday during math, Rachel passed me a note that said, "Did you ask Laurel if she could come to my party?" I wrote back, "Unfortunately, she can't because she just texted me that Sequoia is coming up to hang out with her for the weekend. But I can. That is, if you want me there."

That first part wasn't entirely true. Sequoia was coming up to visit her—but I knew that not because she had texted me, but because Mom had told me and then I read it on WeLoveLaurel.com.

All through the rest of math, and then science and

then English, I kept glancing over at Rachel to see if she was writing me back. Like maybe something along the lines of: "OF COURSE I WANT YOU THERE!!! I've been thinking a lot about it and I realize now that I've been a total jerk and I've missed you soooo much and I'll totally make it up to you for as long as I need to until you forgive me."

But she didn't write that. Or anything else, for that matter. Instead, right before lunch, I saw her crumple up the note and throw it in the garbage as we made our way to the cafeteria.

Instance number 943 where Laurel Moses had yet again ruined my life. I knew it sounded paranoid, but suddenly, I wondered if somehow Laurel had planned this with Rachel. Like somehow she had found out that I told Rachel that we had become friends and she tracked Rachel down and told her it was a lie, but then, at some point during the conversation, they became friends, and now Laurel actually was going to go to the sleepover. It probably wasn't true, but you never knew. And then on Tuesday morning, while Mrs. Kline was yelling for us to settle down, I saw Rachel give Marissa and Cindy their invitations. (I couldn't see exactly what it said, but I did see the big YOU'RE INVITED! on the front). Our social studies assignment that day was "take an action this week that you think will earn you some good karma" (we were studying India, where, like the Buddhists, they're way into karma). If you ask me, the fact that she left me

93

out was very bad karma. As was the idea that Marissa, who was constantly begging me to let her call me her BFF, said she was going to go. Later on, I told Mom what happened, and she said that it sounded like the perfect opportunity to "get a dialogue" going with Rachel and share my feelings and tell her how hurt I was about the whole thing. Frankly, I would rather stick needles in my eye before doing that.

Instead, what I did was go to the girls' room and cry. That is, I went to the girls' room after Noelle Cutrona came up to me and told me I could add her to "The Official Period Log of Sixth-Grade Girls at Jefferson Middle School in Northampton, MA" as the twenty-third girl in the grade to get her period. She had woken up with it that morning, so instead of an exact time, I just wrote "sometime during the night."

Luckily, since being friend-dumped I had gotten really good at crying without sound in the girls' room, so it didn't matter that a few seventh graders came in while I was in there. Plus, I had just refilled my knapsack with the good Kleenex, so when I came out, my nose wasn't all red, and no one could tell. I couldn't believe that instead of being one of three girls in the class not invited to the sleepover, I was now the ONLY one not invited. Talk about embarrassing. How could I have ever been BFFs with someone who would do something that mean?

"Honey, what's the matter?" Dad asked on Friday night as he rewound the rubber band around his ponytail as Sarah, he, and I waited for our pizza at Frankie's. Once when I was overlistening, I heard Grandma Maureen say she thought that the fact that Dad had long hair meant he was unwilling to grow up and be an adult, but here in Northampton, which is full of creative types and hippies, tons of the guys have long hair.

"Nothing," I replied, dragging my breadstick through the oil-and-mustard dip that Dad and I always made when we came here.

"You know, Lucy, I have an essential-oil blend in my bag that might really help with your carbohydrate cravings," Sarah said, flipping her long red braid over her shoulder and rooting around in her bag.

"But I like carbohydrates," I said as I took a bite. "When I eat them, they make me feel better." And when you were forced to spend Friday night with your dad and his girlfriend because everyone else you knew was at a birthday party, you needed something to feel better. I had told Dad all about the Rachel-Laurel-sleepover mess on Wednesday when we played Monopoly. But I asked him not to tell Sarah because I didn't feel like having to sit there while she gave me a bottle of essential oil and said, "Here—put a dab of this on your wrist, and it'll make it so you get your friends back."

"I must have left it at home," she said when she came up empty-handed. I squinted as the light glinted

95

over the little stud in the side of her nose. I wondered if they made you get your nose pierced when you became a yoga teacher, because all of her yoga-teacher friends had them, too. "You know, Lucy, I was just reading an article in Oprah's magazine that said people who talk about their feelings not only get depressed a lot less often, but they also live longer," she said as she took a bite of her boring salad. All that was in it was lettuce and tomatoes. She never got any good stuff like mozzarella cheese or chickpeas. Sarah was very into being healthy and living as long as she could. She once showed me this picture of an old man in one of her yoga magazines and told me he was 122 years old. I do not understand why would you want to live that long, especially since all your friends and family would be long gone and there'd be no one for you to hang out with.

"I know how sad you must feel tonight being the only girl in your class who wasn't invited to the sleepover—" she went on.

"Dad!" I cried, shoving more of my breadstick in my mouth. I couldn't believe he had told her. No, wait—I could. According to Sarah, they told each other everything, which is why they had such a "great relationship."

He reached out and patted my hand. "Honey, I told her so she could share in your pain," he replied.

I didn't even want her sharing my pizza. Not that she would because of the bread thing, I thought as I reached for another breadstick, which made her cringe.

"Girls can be so cruel," she continued. "I mean, I never experienced anything like this when I was young because I was always very popular, but your dad is right. I can feel your pain. When I was doing my yoga-teacher training, there was this one clique of students and I always hoped they'd invite me to go with them for chai tea afterward, but they never did."

As I turned my head toward the door so she wouldn't see me roll my eyes, the door opened and all fifteen girls from Rachel's birthday party and Rachel's mom walked into Frankie's. I bet Sarah could have felt my pain then, because it was like a tidal wave hit me. It wasn't even like I could pretend I didn't see them. They were so loud and giggly and seemed to be having so much fun that you couldn't miss them.

Plus, there was always Marissa to make sure that didn't happen. "Oh! Oh! Look—there's Lucy!" she screeched as they made their way to the back room with the giant long table where people always had their birthday parties—the ones I used to be invited to.

"Hi, Lucy. Hi, Mr. Parker. Hi, Sarah!" she babbled as she stopped at the table. The rest of them went on with only a few "Oh, hey, Lucy"s in passing. Nothing from Rachel or Missy, of course.

"Hi," I mumbled as I slumped down in my chair.

Marissa leaned in close. "Just so you know, I'm not really having a good time," she said in a whisper so loud it might as well have been a yell. "I'm just pretending to have a good time so I won't hurt Rachel's feelings. But since you and I are BFFs, I'd much rather be with you," she said.

"Marissa, are you coming or not?" Rachel called over her shoulder, annoyed.

"Yup! Be right there!" she called back. She turned to me. "Okaywellbyetalktoyoutomorrowloveya!" she said before she ran over to join them.

Yeah, she obviously really wished she were with me.

The only good thing about being totally humiliated in front of an entire restaurant and feeling like even more of a loser was that Dad said that not only could we go to Scoops after dinner, but that I could get whatever I wanted. Even Sarah was nice and didn't say a word about how ice cream wasn't very good for you because of the sugar and dairy and that if I really wanted to be healthy and live longer I'd get some frozen yogurt at Pinkberry around the corner.

I already knew what I was going to get: a large sundae with two scoops (peppermint stick and mint chocolate chip), hot butterscotch and hot caramel, whipped cream, and M&M's. It's kind of a weird combination, which is why I was surprised when I overheard the hoodie-and-sweats-and-sunglasses-(even-though-it-was-eight-thirty-at-night-and-there-was-no-one-in-the-place)-wearing person in front of me ordering the exact same thing.

In fact, I was so surprised, I called out excitedly, "Hey—I'm about to order the same exact same thing!"

And I was even more surprised when the hoodie-and-sweats-and-sunglasses-(even-though-it-was-eight-thirty-at-night-and-no-one-was-in-the-place)-wearing person turned around, put the hoodie down, lifted the sunglasses up, and said, "You are?" It was Laurel—with smudges of chocolate on her face, almost like she had already had a candy bar before coming to Scoops. If I hadn't already spent two (horrible) evenings with her, I probably wouldn't have recognized her because her hair was kind of greasy and in a ponytail and she had no makeup on. Also, her eyes were completely swollen, like she had been crying. But she was Laurel Moses, so it was probably something like allergies or she accidentally poked an eyeliner pencil in her eye or something.

She looked awful, a fact that, although it probably wouldn't help me with the karma thing, made me hate her a little less for ruining my life in so many ways. But when I introduced her to Dad and Sarah, she still put on her movie-star smile and said, "Hi! I'm Laurel! It's so nice to meet you!" By this time, I knew that was what she said to every fan, even though Dad wasn't a fan. He didn't know any of her music since he basically listened only to Bob Dylan, Neil Young, and Crosby, Stills and Nash and he had never seen her show because he only liked to watch documentaries, CNN, and a few shows on HBO. Sarah, however, knew who she was.

After they all said hello and Sarah gushed about how much she loved "Broken Promises," Dad handed me a ten-dollar bill and said, "I think we'll leave you girls alone to eat your sundaes and chat while we go browse in the bookstore for a while."

What was he doing? He knew that the last thing in the world I wanted was to have to be in the same room with her again. In fact, I had complained about it so much that when he picked me up for dinner he said, "Now, Lucy, I don't want to spend all of dinner listening to you complain about Laurel." But before I could say, "Uh, that's okay, I'll just come with you," they were gone.

I ordered my sundae, and Laurel went to sit down at one of the little tables with hers. By the time I joined her, she was almost totally finished

"Wow. I thought I was a fast eater," I said. It was kind of impressive how fast she could shove the ice cream in her mouth.

"Ice cream's the only thing that calms me down," she said with her mouth full. "Fortunately, I have the day off tomorrow, so I can eat it. I can't when I'm working because it makes my face all puffy and then I look like a chipmunk."

"Is that why your eyes are all puffy?" I asked. "From the ice cream?"

She shook her head and her bottom lip started to get a little quivery. Was she going to cry? I sure hoped not, because the last thing I needed was to feel sorry for her. Especially because you couldn't feel sorry for a person and hate them at the same time. And I did hate her.

To stop her from crying, I decided to change the subject. "So where's Sequoia? My mom told me she was coming up to visit you this weekend?" I left out the part that I had also read it on WeLoveLaurel.com so that she didn't think I was a stalker or anything.

Unfortunately, my plan didn't work. Because not only did she start to cry, but she cried so hard that snot came out of her nose and she used the sleeve of her hoodie to wipe if off, even though I offered her a bunch of napkins. I probably would've used my sleeve, too, because the napkins at Scoops are almost as rough as the toilet paper at school.

Just great—some of the hate was evaporating, and I was starting to feel bad for her. Leave it to Laurel to make me feel all confused. "Are you okay?" I asked. I knew it was a dumb question, but it was the only thing I could think of to say. "Do you want me to get you anything?"

She dug out a twenty-dollar bill from her bag. "Maybe another sundae? And get yourself one, too, if you want."

I already felt a little sick from the one I was eating, so I just got one for her. When I came back to the table with hers, she dug into it like she hadn't eaten in ten years.

"So where's Sequoia?" I asked again.

A whole new thing of tears started, making me think that was not the right question to ask.

"S-she d-d-dumped me!" she wailed.

"She did?" I gasped, opening up the napkin container and shoving the entire thing of napkins at her. Laurel Moses had been friend-dumped? How did you friend-dump the most popular girl in the world? That had to be scientifically impossible, right?

She sniffled long and loud. "Yeah. She said she's sick of being friends with someone who's so weird and that she'd rather hang out with Kimber Hernandez." She sniffled again. Kimber Hernandez was the star of *Kimber in the Middle*, the show that came on right after *The World According to Madison Tennyson*. The show was pretty popular, but I thought Kimber was super-cheesy with her extra-tight jeans and really low-cut shirts. Not only that, but she was kind of scary, like mean-scary. She looked like the kind of girl who didn't just threaten to beat other girls up but actually did it.

Laurel wiped her nose with her other sleeve. "So instead of coming up here for the weekend, Sequoia's flying to Miami with Kimber on the Kidz TV private jet, and they're going to hang out at the hotel pool and sneak into clubs even though they're totally underage, and if the Kidz TV people find out, they'll totally get fired."

"Have you been on the Kidz TV jet?" I asked.

She nodded. "Sure. Lots of times."

"I bet they serve really good food on it, huh? Like better than what you get on regular planes."

She thought about it. "I'm not sure. It's been years since I've flown coach, so I have no idea."

Of course she didn't. "But why does Sequoia think you're weird?" I asked. As far as I could tell, the only thing weird about Laurel was that she was freakishly pretty and talented. I mean, sure, she was evil and all, but that wasn't weird.

She shrugged. "I don't know. She says it's because I use so much hand sanitizer. And because I put cotton in my ears when I sleep over at her house because I'm afraid bedbugs might get in them. I also straighten up the stuff in her dressing room as well as mine because of my OCD." She sniffled again. "But I don't think that's so weird. Do you?"

Um, I didn't think that was so weird—it was *really* weird. But I didn't say that. Instead, I just shrugged and said, "No, not really," because I was afraid anything else might make her start crying again. But then, because it was still on my mind, I said, "How do you friend-dump the most popular girl in the world?" and that did make her start crying again.

"You don't have to rub it in!" she wailed. "Although you of all people probably think I deserve it," she said bitterly.

"I'm not trying to rub it in at all!" I said. "It's just that you never think famous people would go through such . . . normal-people things." I shrugged. "Plus, I can't believe we actually have something in common," I said half under my breath.

She wiped her eyes—which, for some reason, after the crying looked even more blue and more pretty. That was kind of unfair. When I cried that hard, I looked like something out of a horror movie. "What do you mean?"

I took a deep breath. I couldn't believe I was about to tell Laurel Moses, my archenemy, about the worst thing ever in my life (except for my parents' divorce, which she already knew about). I launched into the entire story about Missy and Rachel. I had never told anyone—not even Marissa—the entire thing from start to finish. But as I told Laurel everything—from how they didn't even have the decency to do it in person (they three-way called me from the mall so I could barely even hear them) to how, the day of the Hat Incident, I totally recognized their giggles—I realized that, as bad as it had been to have to be the dumpee in the story, it was a very interesting story. It really kept you on the edge of your seat.

For instance, when I was telling her the part about how once, when Missy was volleyball captain in gym class on a day when I had forgotten my Lucy-is-menstruating note, and it was between me and Marissa, I was terrified I'd be the last one chosen, Laurel literally scooted to the edge of hers like it was a movie or something. (Missy may have hated me, but she was also very competitive and knew Marissa was a horrible athlete, which is why she ended up choosing me so I was only second-to-last.)

Finally, I got to this past week, "And then in class the other day, Rachel passed me a note and I opened it very, very, very slowly because I was terrified of what I was about to read..." I didn't, however, tell Laurel about how Rachel had suggested that I bring her with me. Or that I had kinda, sorta given Rachel the impression that Laurel and I were friends at all.

"Oh. My. God," Laurel gasped when I finished describing the nightmare of what had just happened at Frankie's. "Gosh, I haven't even read a script where the story's that awful. Not even the Very Special Episode of my show where Madison gets grounded after she and Sequoia get in a big fight and she writes that thing on the bathroom wall about how Sequoia kissed Jason, even though it's not true, and then gets lectured by her parents about the dangers of spreading rumors."

I had actually seen that episode, and it wasn't half as dramatic as my story.

"You know, you're a really good storyteller. Have you ever thought about writing for television?" she asked.

Wow. That was a big compliment coming from her. "Well, no," I replied. "But I could." Maybe I could create my own series about a girl around my age who has an embarrassing incident every episode.

"You're really brave to even keep going to school. I don't know if I would have the guts to do that," she said.

I shrugged. "Well, hopefully I can be an example for other kids who may be dumped in the future. Kind of like, 'If I can get through it, you can, too.'" I pointed to her sundae. "Hey, do you think I could have a bite of that?" Having to relive the whole friend-drama thing had really zapped my energy.

"Sure," she said, pushing it toward me.

"But you get to be really brave, too," I said, trying not to finish the entire sundae off. "I mean, sure, me having to go through this in Northampton is bad, but for you, if any of those gossip blogs find out about how you were dumped, you'd have to go through it in front of the entire world. That's way more awful than what I'm dealing with."

I honestly meant it as kind of a compliment, but from the terrified look on her face, I realized she hadn't thought about that part yet. Before I could apologize, the bell on the door tinkled and the hair on the back of my neck stood up. I looked over and realized that the next chapter in my very dramatic story was about to be written. The entire slumber party came barreling through the door.

"That's them!" I whispered to Laurel. I felt like I was in this very funny movie *Groundhog Day* I had once seen where the guy just keeps having the same day over and over again. Except my *Groundhog Day* wasn't funny. My *Groundhog Day* was a sixth-grader horror movie.

I tried to slide down in my seat, like I had in the pizza place, but because Laurel and I were the only customers in there (it was February and super-cold, after all), I couldn't exactly hide. Laurel at least could put her hoodie up and her sunglasses on, and that's exactly what she did.

Then Marissa saw me. There was no going back now. "Omigosh! Look, guys—Lucy's here! That's twice in one night!" Marissa announced, loudly, to the group before she came rushing over.

Could this night get any worse? I could feel the ice cream moving up from my stomach into my throat.

"Hey, Lucy! Whatcha doing?" she asked, leaning in close. I just wanted to crawl under the table and hide. "Where's your dad? Who's this?"

"Uh—" The ice cream moved up even more.

Laurel tried to duck her head, but Marissa was too fast for her and peered closer. Marissa gave the loudest gasp in the history of gasps. "Oh. My. God. Laurel Moses!" she screeched. "I'd recognize that silver heart necklace anywhere—it's the one you're wearing in the *Fun in the Sun: Madison on Spring Break* movie poster!"

Fifteen heads from over at the ice-cream counter whipped around at the same time. If I threw up in front of all these people, I was definitely going to have to change schools.

"Why are you wearing sunglasses inside when it's nighttime?" Marissa demanded. "You know, I heard you can go blind doing that."

"Um—" Laurel started to say.

"She's wearing them because she had a really bad

allergy attack because by mistake there was a little piece of peanut on her sundae so her eyes got all swollen, and because of that the light hurts them and if she doesn't keep them on, she might go blind," I finished for her.

Laurel's shoulders dropped from her ears as she gave me a grateful smile. She may have been a great karaoker, but being able to come up with really good lies on the spot was one of *my* talents.

"I didn't know you were allergic to peanuts!" Marissa said. "It's not in the One Hundred Random Facts About Laurel section of your website." She thrust out her hand. "Anyway, I'm Marissa Parini, Lucy's best friend." Marissa looked at me and must have seen the expression of horror on my face. "I used to be her third best friend, but when Rachel and Missy—who are right over there, by the way—dumped her, I got to move up. Missy's the one with braces and Rachel's the one whose face is kinda shiny because she's got oily skin."

Yup, the throwing-up part was probably going to be here any second.

"Anyway," Marissa continued, reaching into her back pocket, "I've been carrying this around for weeks, just in case I ran into you," she said, shoving a folded-up picture of Laurel from her Official Laurel Moses Fan Club Welcome Kit. "It's a little warm because I've been sitting on it, but maybe you can sign it? Maybe write 'To my very good friend Marissa. With tons of love from her very good friend, Laurel'?"

"Uh...sure," Laurel said, digging in her bag for a pen as the rest of the girls just stood there frozen like they were in the middle of a game of Statues.

"Ooh, ooh! I know. And because it's Rachel's birthday tomorrow, maybe you could write 'Happy Birthday' to her!" She grabbed a napkin off the table. "Like on this napkin." She turned. "Hey, Rachel—come here and meet Laurel Moses! She's going to write 'Happy Birthday' on a napkin for you!"

Because Rachel and Missy traveled only as a unit—always RachelandMissy instead of just Rachel or Missy (or RachelMissyandLucy)—the two of them came over to our table together.

"Guys, this is Laurel Moses," said Marissa, flinging her arm around Laurel's shoulder. "Laurel, this is Rachel and Missy."

"Hi," they said shyly, not even looking at me, even though I was standing right there.

Even though only minutes before she had been bawling her eyes out, Laurel still managed to put on her movie-star smile and said, "Hi! I'm Laurel! It's so nice to meet you!" I was great at lying on the spot, but even if I went to acting school for years, I don't think I'd ever be able to pretend like nothing was wrong nearly as well as Laurel.

Rachel turned to me. "I thought you said the reason you guys couldn't come to my sleepover was because Sequoia was coming to visit and she was going to hang out with her."

Now I was definitely going to throw up. I'd left that part out of my super-dramatic retelling on purpose. Once Laurel found out I had lied and I'd told Rachel that I'd bring her to the party, she'd totally hate me. Especially since, now that she knew the whole story, she'd know that I was doing it only in order to try to get Rachel and Missy to be my friends again. And once they found out that Laurel knew nothing about the sleepover up until a few minutes ago, that was never going to happen.

I racked my brain for something, anything. But nothing came up. All that came out was "Uhhhh—"

"She was going to come up," Laurel said, "but then I decided that I'd rather hang out with Lucy than her. If you want to know the truth, Lucy's a lot more fun than Sequoia is."

By this time the rest of the girls had sort of gathered around, and, in stereo, all of their jaws dropped. Including mine.

Missy's eyes bugged out, which because they were buggy to begin with, made her look really weird. "You'd rather hang out with Lucy than another famous star?" she gasped.

"Well, yeah," Laurel replied, as if Missy had just asked the dumbest question in the entire world. "Wouldn't you?" she said.

Missy didn't say anything. Probably because her jaw dropped even more, making it impossible for her to talk.

Laurel turned to me and, without anyone seeing, gave me a little wink. Because of my coordination problem I didn't risk trying to wink back, but I did smile. I didn't know how the Academy Awards voting thing worked, but Laurel deserved one for this performance. She made it seem totally believable that she meant every word.

chapter 9

Dear Dr. Maude,

I don't have a lot of time to write because I'm about to go to the mall with LAUREL MOSES of all people, if you can believe it. Dad's not done meditating yet, so I thought I'd check my e-mail first (a) to see if you had written back by any chance and (b) to ask you another question.

I won't go into it now because it's kind of a long story, but basically, A LOT happened last night. First of all, I found out that Laurel was dumped by HER BFF, too, which made me feel (a) sorry for her and (b) kind-of, sort-of like her. And THEN she completely saved my life when I was about to be totally humiliated by Rachel and Missy in front of all the girls in my class at this ice-cream place which made me like her even more. So because (a) neither of us has plans today and (b) I have this assignment for social studies class where I have to do something to earn good karma, I decided to ask her if she wanted to go to the mall so I could show her what it was like to have a regular day doing regular kid things.

I have a feeling I've already started earning karma points, because she was so excited about the idea, you would've thought I asked her if she wanted to go to Paris or something.

And then after that I blurted out, "Hey, do you think our parents went away this weekend to get engaged, because Marissa says that when people go away for two nights it's because they're getting engaged?" Well, she got all pale and then she said, "You know, I hadn't thought about that, but now that you bring it up, I did overhear my dad talking to his best friend, Larry, on the phone, and he said that things were getting pretty serious with the woman he was dating."

This is what I was afraid of, Dr. Maude. I don't listen to Marissa a lot of the time because of the lying thing. But I do find it a little weird that her mother said the SAME EXACT THING—"Things are getting serious"—to Marissa right before she got engaged to Phil, Marissa's stepdad.

Is this true—that if a person says that things are getting serious, it means they're going to propose? I really hope not because maybe Laurel's not that bad, but, still, it doesn't mean I'm ready for her to be my STEPSISTER!!

If you could PLEASE write back and let me know, I'd really appreciate it.

yours truly,
LUCY B. PARKER

Before we could go have a normal day at the mall, we had to go through Laurel's clothes and find her a normal-girl outfit. Because she had two huge closets full, you'd think that would be easy, but it wasn't. Everything she had was more eighth-grade-formal rather than lunch-at-the-Food-Court-like.

As I ix-nayed every item she held up (a fake fur-collared sweater, a suede skirt) and she told me a little bit about her very not-normal life, I started feeling even more sorry for her (which seemed to make it so I hated her less and liked her more). Sure, she got to do very cool things like go to the MTV Movie Awards, but a lot of her life was just plain sad. First of all, she didn't have any pets because she was as weird about pet hair as she was about germs ("But you like Miss Piggy! And you could have a fish—they don't have hair," I suggested, even though I knew from the one time I had had a fish that they were pretty boring). And I was right about the bowling thing. Well, almost right. She had been bowling, just once, but it was at the White House before the president got rid of the bowling alley and replaced it with a basketball court. I didn't ask, but I bet they had a whole supply of new shoes that had never been worn there.

"So where do people have their birthday parties in New York?" I asked as I gave a thumbs-down to a pair of jeans with rhinestones on the butt pockets. Jeans were fine for the Holyoke Mall, but just plain ones. "Ice-skating rinks? Miniature golf?" I asked, even though as soon as the words came out, I realized the idea of a miniature golf course in the middle of a city was weird.

"Well, last year for Jaycee's birthday, I took her to Two Bunch Palms in California," she replied, holding up a long leather jacket that, when I touched it, I found was as soft as butter. Jaycee was her assistant.

I shook my head no as I took the jacket from her and threw it back on the bed. "What's Two Bunch Palms?"

"A spa with massages and facials and stuff."

That sounded like the most boring place in the entire world to spend a birthday. "But what about your real friends?" I asked. "The ones you go to school with." I knew from her website that since kindergarten, Laurel had gone to this place in New York called Professional Children's School, where all the kids there were dancers or other actors. Not that I was stalking her or anything.

As she held up a pink cashmere sweater, I nodded. I had a red cashmere one that I was only allowed to wear on special occasions, but by this time the choosing-a-normal-girl outfit was getting boring, so I decided it would have to do.

"Sequoia was pretty much my only friend. Because of the show, I'm barely at school anymore," she said. "If I'm not taping the series, I'm away shooting a movie or recording an album."

"That's a lot of work," I said.

She shrugged. "I guess. But because it started when I was six, I'm just used to it by now."

I knew from a documentary Dad had once rented that kids in other countries started working when they were really young because they were so poor, but this was America and Laurel was rich.

"And when I am at school, everyone treats me weird," she went on.

"But how come? I mean, if the other kids are actors, too."

She shrugged again. "Because I'm really famous and the other ones mostly do commercials or maybe a soap opera here or there."

Looking through one of her closets, I found a pair of nonsequined jeans and threw them on the bed next to the pink sweater. It would've been a little better if they had had a pen mark or a ketchup stain somewhere on them, instead of having creases down the leg because they had been ironed, but they'd do. "Okay, but who do you eat lunch with when you are there?" I asked. Everyone at least had a lunch friend. Even after the friend-dumping, I had Marissa. It wasn't saying much, but it was something.

"I know you're going to think I'm a total loser when I tell you this," she replied, "but I usually just bring my sandwich into the girls' room and eat there. Luckily it's really clean."

That was one of the saddest things I had ever heard. "But you're still a teenager," I said. "You have to have some fun. Don't you have any hobbies or anything?" I just hoped she didn't say African drumming because I had decided the other night that that was something I might want to try out, and I didn't need her being better than me at that, too.

She thought about it. "I like to read."

Eating in the girls' room? Spending her free time reading? It was like she had the same exact life as Maeve O'Connor, the least popular girl at Jefferson.

"Well, that sounds . . . fun," I lied. Maybe Laurel wasn't as stuck-up as I had originally thought. Maybe she was just shy or didn't have a lot of social skills because, when you took away the big-star part, she was just . . . lonely. You didn't read that on the blogs.

And, since being dumped, loneliness was definitely something I knew about.

Yet another thing we had in common.

Even in the pink sweater and jeans, Laurel still looked too Laurel, which is why as a last resort we ran down to the hotel gift shop and bought her a pair of sweats and an oversized blechy gray Northampton sweatshirt. But even with that she still needed more of a disguise so there wasn't a stampede if people recognized her. Because someone getting trampled and crushed to death in front of Target would not have been a typical Saturday afternoon at the mall.

It was time to call in the big guns—Roger and Maya.

Roger, her hair guy, and Maya, her makeup woman, were used to making her look beautiful and glamorous, but making her look like just one more Holyoke Mall–goer on a Saturday afternoon was harder.

"What do you think?" Roger asked Maya and me, after he adjusted the short red bob wig on Laurel's head. I was sitting at the piano picking out a not-very-good version of "Chopsticks" and trying not to stare at Roger's arms too much. His arms were completely covered in tattoos, to the point where you couldn't even see any skin. "Chopsticks" was easy, but because of my coordination problem, and the staring thing, I kept hitting the wrong keys.

Maya sat on the sofa, chugging a disgusting-smelling green drink from the health-food store that she said kept her really healthy. I bet she and Sarah would get along really well. "Still too glamorous," she said, shaking her head.

Roger threw his hands up. "Girl, you are working my last nerve! This is the fifth wig you've had me pull out." I thought at first that Roger didn't like me, but when he was in the bathroom, Maya told me not to worry—that he was a total drama queen and just came off as sarcastic and almost a little mean. He turned to me. "And you are hurting my eardrums."

I stopped. "Sorry," I said. "What about that one?" I asked, pointing to a long brown wavy one. It reminded me of my hair before I burned it all off, but with pretty curls instead of frizz.

He exchanged the bob for the curls and turned Laurel to us again. "Better?"

We nodded. "Much," said Maya.

"But if you want her to look more like a normal girl, I'd brush it a little so it doesn't look so perfect," I suggested. "Maybe give her a little hat head or a rat's nest or something."

Roger's eyes narrowed. "There will be absolutely no rat's nests on my watch," he announced. "I know—we'll add a hat!" he said, reaching over and plucking the Boston Celtics baseball hat off my head and plopping it on Laurel's.

"Omigod!" Laurel gasped as her hands flew up, batting the hat away as if it were a bug.

"Hey! What are you doing?!" I yelped, clamping my hands on top of my head. Maybe they were used to seeing weird-looking people in New York City, which is why, unlike the crowd outside the bookstore that day, Roger and Maya weren't staring at me like I was an alien, but still—that kind of behavior was just plain rude. "I need my hat back!"

Roger didn't even apologize or listen to me. He turned to Laurel and said, very calmly, "Laurel, sweetheart, the germ-phobia stuff is getting a little tiresome. Just keep the hat on long enough to get some hat head. It's not even on your real hair." Then he turned to me and raised an eyebrow. "Ah. So that's why you're wearing a hat," he said. "Honey, who gave you that haircut?"

"My godmother, Deanna," I mumbled as I stood there with my arms and legs wrapped around myself as if, instead of just being hatless, I was completely naked.

"You. Sit here." He pointed at the chair next to Laurel, who, with her eyes shut, was holding her breath while she waited for the hat head to cook while Maya took some tubes and brushes out of what looked like a piece of carry-on luggage and started painting some fake pimples on her forehead. He reached over and started messing with my hair, making the *tsk-tsk* sound my grandmother made whenever she saw Mom leaving the house without lipstick. "Note to self: this is why a person should always go to a trained professional."

"She is a trained professional," I replied. "She's got her own salon and everything."

"Maybe with a degree from Supercuts," he muttered. He reached for a comb and a pair of scissors. "May I?"

Roger was a little intimidating. I was too scared to say no, so I looked at Laurel, who nodded. I nodded, too.

Finally, Laurel exhaled. "Huh. This isn't so bad," she announced. "I don't feel like I'm going to have a panic attack or anything." She didn't? If that was what "normal" looked like for her, I'd hate to see how she acted when she was having a panic attack.

Roger combed and snipped, and Maya and Laurel made lots of "I like that" and "Oh, that looks great" comments, which made me less nervous. When he was done, he turned my head to face them. "Okay, peanut gallery—what do you think?"

"I love it!" said Maya. "It's utterly and completely rad." Coming from a person who had streaks of pink in her hair, I wasn't sure it was a good thing that she loved it so much.

"You look like a totally different person," Laurel said.

"Like how different are we talking about?" I asked nervously. I know Mom wanted Laurel and me to get along, but I didn't think she'd be too happy if she couldn't recognize her own daughter anymore.

Roger handed me a mirror. "See for yourself."

"Wow," I said. Obviously it was still short, but somehow the choppy layers helped to make it seem fuller and longer, and the wispy bangs made it a lot less egg-looking and a lot more girly-looking. It was both cute and sophisticated at the same time, which is a very good combination.

Laurel studied me. "Hmm. You know, with your new haircut, just a little bit of makeup would really show off your amazing bone structure and make your eyes totally pop." Before the word *pop* had even fully left her mouth, Maya had more brushes out and was fiddling with some palettes of colored powder.

"I'm on it," Maya said.

"Is that okay?" Laurel asked me.

I nodded nervously. Mom would freak if she knew I was wearing makeup, but she was so busy with Alan in New York falling in love or getting engaged or something, she probably wouldn't even notice. Like Missy and Rachel had brought up during the dumping, I was not a fan of makeup. Maybe I would've liked it more if the one time I wore it—when Missy's mom had a Mary Kay cosmetics lady come to Missy's birthday sleepover and give us all makeovers—hadn't been such a traumatic experience. I'm pretty sure the woman was drunk, because not only did she leave me looking like a clown, but she also poked me in the eye a bunch of times with the eye pencil. The minute she was done, I washed it off and hadn't gone near the stuff since (except for the Smith's Rosebud Salve Strawberry Lip Balm).

"Maya, maybe some of the Summer Shimmer highlighter on her cheekbones I wore at the Emmys last year?" Laurel suggested. "And the Smoky Sable liner around her eyes, like we did for the Grammys? Oh, and that Screen Siren lip gloss I wore at the Tonys?" Maya brushed and painted away and Laurel continued to call out suggestions ("Maybe smudge the liner just a little more." "I'd skip the lip pencil so she doesn't look like one of those pageant girls."). If the acting thing ever stopped working for her, she could totally get a job doing makeovers at one of the makeup counters in Macy's. In addition to acting, singing, and dancing, she could add "knows a lot about makeup" to the list of the gazillion things she was good at.

Maya stood back and turned to Laurel. "Thoughts?"

"Perfect," Laurel said.

Maya stared at me for a second. "Can I pluck your eyebrows a little bit?" she asked.

"No!" I yelped. The last thing I needed was to lose any

more hair. Plus, I knew from the way Mom winced when she did her own that it hurt. I was not ready for that.

"Okay, okay," she said, handing me a mirror. "So what do you think?"

This was nothing like the clown makeup the Mary Kay lady had put on. When I looked in the mirror, I totally understood why women wasted time that could've been spent sleeping a few extra minutes in the morning putting on makeup and then walking around with gunk on their faces all day long. When a real, nondrunk makeup artist who specialized in Hollywood stars did it, it made a huge difference. Thanks to the blush, my face, which was pretty round (back when I lost my first front tooth, I looked like a jack-o'-lantern) looked a lot thinner, and you could see that I had actual cheekbones. The eyeliner made my green eyes look super-green and super-big (but not so big that I looked bug-eyed, like Marissa). And if I had had any interest in kissing a boy, my lips looked very kissable.

Roger put his arm around Maya. "Oh, I never cease to amaze myself with our brilliance."

"You look awesome," agreed Laurel.

"Thanks," I said with a smile. I looked at her. "And I hope you don't take this the wrong way or anything, but you look awful."

"I do?!" she asked with her own smile. "Thanks." In her wig, the sweatshirt, the fake pimples, and the pair of Maya's plain-lens glasses she had just put on, you'd never know that Laurel Moses was Laurel Moses.

In fact, with my makeover and her makeunder, you could almost now believe the two of us might be kind-of, sort-of friends. I mean, we weren't friends-friends yet, because you had to spend quality time with them at a mall or a sleepover to see what they were really like, but this was definitely a start.

Luckily, Dad was really distracted when he drove us to the mall. He didn't say anything about my makeup or the fact that Laurel looked like a total dweeb. (Not that he would've said anything about that last part because it would've been rude.) He was so out of it, I had to poke him and ask, "Um, Dad, do you notice anything different about me by any chance?" before he picked up on the fact that I wasn't wearing a hat for the first time in five months.

When we got to the mall, it was filled with the usual weekend crowd of giggling bunches of BFFs. It had been a long time since I had been there on a Saturday, because after the friend-dumping, there was no way I was going to embarrass myself by showing up there with a parent and possibly running into Rachel and Missy. And there was definitely no way I was going to show up with Marissa, even though she asked me to go every week. In fact, when I asked her what she wanted for her birthday back in December, she said all she wanted was for me to go to the mall with her on a Saturday so we could do BFF things like try on bras together. I didn't tell her that I would cut all my hair off completely before I tried on bras, with her or anyone else. Plus, the kind of BFFs-at-the-mall things I liked to do were more like going into stores and pretending I didn't speak English or had just escaped from a mental hospital. At least that's what Rachel and Missy and I used to do.

I had to admit it felt pretty good to be back there on a prime mall-going day, even if (a) I was there with someone who was only a potential kind-of, sort-of friend and (b) that person kept stopping every five steps to take another picture with her phone's camera. Seriously, you would've thought we were in Africa on safari or some other crazy exotic location the way she was acting. Especially when we got to the Food Court.

"You know, I think there's a brochure of the mall you can get at the information desk that has a bunch of pictures of the Food Court in there," I said as she snapped a photo of the Orange Julius. This was getting a little embarrassing.

"Ooh—look! Free samples!" she said excitedly, pointing to a tray of baked pretzels over at Uncle Tim's. "Let's get some," she said, dragging me over.

Wow. Who knew Laurel Moses liked free samples? Maybe she was more of a regular kid than I had thought.

"So you really haven't been to a mall since you got famous?" I asked after we finished our first samples and tried to nonchalantly take seconds without the woman with the wart behind the counter yelling at us.

"Well, when my book *The World of Style According to Madison Tennyson* came out, I did a signing at the Time Warner Center in New York, but they don't have a food court, so I don't know if it's technically a mall."

I shook my head. "Nope. It needs a food court to be a mall."

"Then no," she said, reaching for a third sample. Gosh, she was brave. I had been yelled at by Wart Lady for double-sampling before, and it was not fun. "I haven't."

"But then how do you get your clothes?" I asked.

"Zoë brings them to me," she replied, hiding her hand behind her back when Wart Lady whipped around and gave us a dirty look.

"Who's Zoë?"

She reached for a fourth sample. Was she crazy?! Luckily, Wart Lady was now busy helping a woman who kept pointing through the glass and saying, "No—not that pretzel there. That pretzel there." "Zoë is my stylist. See, designers want you to wear their stuff so it ends up in pictures in magazines and they get free publicity, so they give it to Zoë, and she gives it to me."

"And you don't have to pay for it?"

"Sometimes. But a lot of the time, no."

Wow. If I had a stylist, I would've had her call Converse to see if they could send me over sneakers in every color. "And this is, like, nice stuff—not like T.J. Maxx or Marshalls stuff, huh?" I asked.

"Who's T.J. Maxx?" she asked, snapping a picture of the pizza place.

Okay, maybe she wasn't that regular.

Laurel may not have been regular, but she was funny. I had always liked the sorry-but-we-don't-speak-English part of the day at the mall with Rachel and Missy, but it was even more fun with Laurel because she could do all these great accents, including a French one that cracked me up so much I almost peed in my pants. (I'm pretty sure a few drops actually came out, but I just couldn't help it.)

Thankfully, my plan to keep her undercover was working great. Her voice may have been a little recognizable, but the rest of the disguise made it so that none of the other shoppers had any clue who she was. If they looked at her twice, it was only because she looked like a dork. As we walked past Barbara's Bra World on our way to Target, I cringed. The humiliation of being told I was going to be very busty when I grew up was still fresh in my mind.

"Lucy, you're totally right—Target is totally epic!" Laurel announced as we browsed the racks of purses.

"I know. Wait till you see H&M—that's pretty great, too," I said.

She held up a red bag with buckles and gasped as she looked at the price. "I can't believe this is only $14.99—it looks just like my Marc Jacobs one, and that cost over a thousand dollars!" She grabbed the red one, and also grabbed it in blue, green, and black. She turned to me. "Want one?"

I shook my head. I wasn't that into purses. I hardly ever carried one, which was another reason Rachel and Missy had given as to why they didn't want to be my friend.

"Oh, okay. Hey, I was thinking . . . I'd really like to buy you a present."

"A present? For what? It's not my birthday for another 284 days." I didn't have OCD tendencies like Laurel did, but I couldn't wait to turn thirteen. I had already marked off the days on the calendar on my bedroom wall. A lot of girls I knew (Rachel, Missy, Marissa) couldn't wait, because it meant they were that much closer to wearing makeup, or shaving their legs, or doing stuff like that. For me, all that seemed more like a pain in the butt than fun. But when you told someone your age and there was a "teen" after it—thirteen, fourteen—you were taken more seriously. At least that's what I was hoping.

"For, you know, hanging out with me," she replied. She started digging in her purse for her wallet. "Or, if you want, I could just write you a check and you could save the money for something else you want."

"Wait a minute—you think you have to pay me to

hang out with you?" I asked as I ran my hand through my hair for like the billionth time since Roger had cut it. It was so freeing not to be wearing a hat.

She shrugged. "I don't know...yeah?"

Okay, that was just completely sad and weird at the same time. The more I talked to Laurel, the more I felt like she didn't live on earth but inside a television set. She was able to sing in front of an entire Super Bowl crowd, but when it came to living in the real world, she pretty much had no clue. If she was as annoying as Marissa, then I could see why she might feel the need to pay someone to be her friend, but she wasn't. In fact, even though I kept waiting for her to do something that made me have to hate her again, she hadn't. It was up to me to show her how friends really worked.

"Um, that's not how it works," I replied. "I know you have an assistant, and a stylist, and a therapist, and the woman who comes over and gives you massages, and all those other people in your life, but, see, friends hang out with you just because...well, because they want to. Not because you pay them with checks or roles on TV shows or gifts when it's not their birthday."

"So, you and I...we're, like...officially friends now?" she asked shyly.

I wasn't sure how to respond. People didn't usually ask each other if they were friends—they just realized one day that they were.

"You're not just doing all this because my dad is

dating your mom, and because things are getting serious and we might one day be stepsisters?" she went on.

I cringed. I was trying very hard to forget that part. "Well, obviously if they weren't, then we probably never would have met because you're famous and I'm not," I said, "and you sort of have to spend a lot of time with a person until you're really friends, but what you did last night at the ice-cream place in front of Rachel and Missy, and how you let Roger and Maya do my hair and makeup? Those are definitely friend things to do. And spending the day at the mall together is also a friendlike event," I went on, "so, yeah, I guess you'd say we're becoming friends. That is, you know, if you want to be..."

"Yeah, I want to be," she said with a smile before walking over to the accessories section and picking up some bobby pins with rhinestone butterflies on the end. "But even if we're friends, I'm still buying these for you because they'll look totally cute with your new haircut. I may not have a lot of experience with the friend thing, but I do know how to accessorize."

After Target we went to H&M so we could play TWUO, which stands for The World's Ugliest Outfit. It was a game that Rachel and Missy and I had made up in fourth grade, and I had really missed it. It wasn't like I could play it with Marissa. Because she dressed in weird ugly outfits every day, she wouldn't get the joke. Also, I didn't want to admit she was my friend, because, well, she's Marissa. Because the clothes in H&M were so cool, it was a lot harder to play TWUO there, rather than, say, the Misses Department at Marshalls. Either way, you could never go wrong with sequins or rhinestones. Which is exactly why Marissa was a bad choice—she wore at least one rhinestone thing every day of her life.

We broke up in the store to make our choices, then met up at the dressing rooms. I thought the outfit I concocted was pretty good (and by good, I mean horrible): orange tube top with little mirrored squares all over it, a hot pink wool miniskirt, and a polka-dot headband. But when Laurel opened her dressing room door, the combination of a red-and-black-striped turtleneck, zebra-print skirt, a purple shrug, and a leopard scarf was so ugly it almost made me want to throw up. That or laugh, especially because her wig was all crooked. She looked in the mirror, and we both cracked up.

"You definitely won," I said after I could finally stand up straight again. My stomach hurt from laughing so hard.

"I don't know—orange is pretty bad," she replied, wiping her eyes. "The only time I was ever on one of those Fashion Disaster lists, it was because I was wearing an orange dress."

"Yeah, but mixing animal prints always wins," I replied. I was impressed, she was even good at being ugly—was there anything Laurel Moses wasn't good at?

Suddenly, I heard a shrill voice. "Omigod—I can't believe it! Lucy, what are you doing at the mall on a Saturday?! You hate coming to the mall on weekends!"

Marissa.

Laurel and I looked at each other, panicked. Just what we needed—the biggest mouth in all of Northampton had spotted us, and was probably ready to blab that Laurel Moses was in the dressing room of H&M wearing the ugliest outfit in the history of ugly outfits.

I turned around. "Marissa, what are you doing here?" I asked nervously, stepping in front of Laurel to try to hide her and her winning ugly outfit. "Weren't all you guys from the sleepover going to the movies?"

"We were supposed to, but the only thing non-R-rated that wasn't sold out was *Barking My Way Back to You*, and no one except me wanted to see it, so we're shopping instead," she replied. "Hey, who's that behind you?"

"Ahh ... this is ... my cousin," I said, trying to push Laurel back into the dressing room.

"What are you talking about? You don't have any cousins," she said, confused. "Remember, we had to do that family-tree assignment last year and you didn't have any cousins and everyone thought that was really weird?"

"What I meant was that I didn't have any American cousins," I said. "This is ... my French cousin, Dominique."

"Bonjour!" said Laurel, popping out from behind me. She leaned over to pick up the glasses that had fallen off her face when I pushed her behind me, and her wig shifted. Oh no. This was not good. If the disguise went, we were in big trouble.

Marissa gasped. "Omigod—you're from France?!" She moved closer and started yelling very slowly. "DO YOU SPEAK ENGLISH?" she yelled. "OH, AND I LOVE YOUR OUTFIT! YOU FRENCH PEOPLE HAVE THE BEST TASTE IN CLOTHES! CAN YOU UNDERSTAND ME?"

"Nope—she doesn't," I said, stepping backward to put some distance between us and Marissa. I heard a loud crunching sound—I had stepped on the glasses. Uh-oh. My coordination problem was not helping things. "And now she can't see, either, so you should probably just go away now, Marissa, because there's no use for you to try and talk to a person who can't see or understand you."

Marissa ran to the edge of the dressing room. "Hey, you guys! Come here!" she yelled out into the store. "Lucy's here with her cousin from France who doesn't speak a word of English—you have to come meet her!"

I sighed. Everything had been going so well up until now. I wondered if I had been born with some gene that made it so no matter what, things in my life were bound to blow up. I looked down and saw that Laurel's wig had somehow managed to get so loose that it had almost completely turned around so that the long part was in her eyes and the bangs were on the side of her head.

Marissa turned around and spotted Laurel fixing her wig. "Wait a minute—that's not your cousin!" she gasped. "That's Laurel!" She ran back to the entrance of the dressing room before I could stop her. "You guys! It's not Lucy's cousin—it's Laurel Moses!" she yelled out. "You have to come see her—she has the most awesome outfit on!"

Laurel and I looked at each other. This was a nightmare. "Now what?" she panicked. "I can't have pictures of me dressed like this get out there!"

"Quick—get back in the dressing room!" I yelled.

She ran back to her dressing room to hide before the entire sleepover came rushing in. Except somehow the door had gotten jammed and she couldn't get it shut. Before we could get her into an empty room, the stampede of girls showed up, all with their cell-phone cameras and digital cameras whipped out and pointed our way.

"Hey—no pictures!" I yelled.

Like anyone was really going to listen to me. As the sound of clicking cameras filled the air, Laurel and I were momentarily blinded.

When I could see again, I grabbed her and pulled her into another dressing room.

"Well, I guess that's the end of our regular day at the mall," I sighed. "It was fun while it lasted."

Outside, we could hear a packed dressing room full of girls screaming things like, "Hey, Laurel, can I have an autograph?" "Can I get a picture with you?" I just hoped when we finally left the dressing room, no one got trampled to death.

As I stood there looking at her, in her ugly outfit and her crooked wig, I couldn't help it—I started to laugh. She just looked so . . . awful. Thankfully, instead of saying something like, "Oh, so that's what a friend does? She laughs?" she started to laugh, too. We laughed so hard that I had to cross my legs so I didn't pee.

Which is something that often happens when you're hanging out with a friend.

chapter 10

DEAR DR. MAUDE,

OKAY, I REALLY, REALLY, REALLY NEED YOUR HELP, WHICH IS WHY I AM WRITING IN ALL CAPS. OVER THE LAST FEW DAYS IT'S LIKE MY LIFE WAS PUT INTO THE MICROWAVE AND NO ONE BOTHERED TO POKE A FEW HOLES IN THE WRAPPER ON TOP OF IT, AND IT JUST COMPLETELY EXPLODED ALL OVER THE PLACE.

I WON'T GO INTO ALL OF IT NOW, BECAUSE IT'S A VERY LONG STORY, BUT DO YOU THINK THAT MAYBE YOU COULD SEND ME YOUR PHONE NUMBER AND I COULD CALL YOU AND TALK TO YOU ABOUT IT? I CAN'T TALK TO MY PARENTS ABOUT IT, SINCE THEY'RE PART OF IT. BUT I PROMISE I WON'T GIVE YOUR NUMBER TO ANYONE ELSE.

yours truly,
Lucy B. Parker

I think it's completely unfair how whoever is in charge of running the universe makes it so a really nice day—

complete with a new haircut and a makeover—can turn into one of the worst nights of your entire life.

I should've known that it was going to be bad when, after Dad got us from the mall security office, where the mall cops made Laurel and me wait, and we had dropped Laurel off at her hotel, Dad said, "I was thinking we'd go to India House for dinner, just the two us." (a) We had just gone out for dinner last night, and Dad was an artist so it wasn't like we could afford to go out for dinner too many times in a row. Especially if we were going to India House, which was kind of expensive. And (b) Wednesday was our usual "quality time alone" night, not Saturday. Non-Wednesday nights he liked to include Sarah, so she and I could bond. Something was definitely up. Was I in trouble for causing a riot at the mall? And, if so, it was a little unfair that Laurel wasn't getting in trouble, too, because she was just as responsible.

But when the naan and raita arrived at our table, Dad looked at me all seriously, and he said, "We need to have a Talk." Uh-oh. Everyone knew that Talks-with-capital-Ts were not good. In fact, in my experience, they usually ended in groundings of some sort. Or, if not groundings, at least serious warnings with the threat of groundings.

"We didn't mean to end up almost causing a stampede in H&M! Laurel and I were just hanging out, and things got…a little out of hand." Or a lot, in the H&M manager's opinion. "But we were bonding! Like Mom wanted! And it's not like I wore the makeup to school," I cried. "The reason I let Maya put it on was because for once in my life I wanted to know what it felt like to be pretty," I confessed. "Especially when I was going to be spending the day with someone who's considered one of the most beautiful people in the world."

"Huh? What are you talking about, Lucy?" Dad asked, all confused.

"Wait, what? Weren't you going to yell at me about the makeup I have on? Or the stampede at the mall?" I asked, equally confused.

"What makeup?"

"Oh. Never mind," I said.

But the Talk-with-a-capital-*T* ended up not being about something I had done. It was about something he and Sarah had done when they "did it."

"Lucy, you may have noticed that Sarah's been acting a little weird lately," he said.

What I wanted to say was, "Uh, Dad, I have a newsflash for you—she's always weird," but I didn't. Instead, I said, "Not particularly."

"You haven't noticed she's been really tired, and careful about what she eats?"

Um, maybe she was tired because she did yoga like twenty hours a day? And she was always careful about what she ate.

I shook my head.

"Well, she has. And the reason for that is because she's pregnant."

"Pregnant?!" I cried. "As in I'm-going-to-be-a-SISTER pregnant?

He nodded, a huge grin on his face.

"But . . . you're not even married yet," I said, dazed.

"Lucy, lots of people have babies with their partners without being legally married," he replied. "You know that. Half your friends' parents aren't married."

"Yeah, but that's them," I said.

"As Sarah likes to say, although our union may not be recognized in the eyes of the government, we're fully committed to each other on a soul level," he said.

I rolled my eyes. Great—he was starting to sound as weird as Sarah did. And now that they were having a baby together, he'd probably stop eating bread and become totally obsessed with living as long as he could. And I wasn't even going to begin to think about how weird the baby would be or what sort of strange name Sarah would want to give it. "Wait—so you really mean pregnant in the sense of I'm-going-to-be-a-sister pregnant?" I asked again. "Not . . . I don't know . . . a different kind of pregnant?"

"Yup. Isn't that exciting?" he asked.

Uh, no. It was not exciting. It was awful. Thank goodness I was wearing a pad, because the total and complete shock of finding out that I was going to be a sister had to be enough to bring on my period. (Unfortunately, when I went to the bathroom a little later to check, there was nothing, which was beyond unfair.

I mean, if you were going to make someone have to listen to news that was going to completely change her life forever, something good should've come out of it.)

"We weren't trying to get pregnant," he went on, "but Sarah doesn't like to take birth control pills because all these studies have shown that they're not sure what they do to your health, and she has an allergic reaction to the latex in condoms—"

"Dad! Gross!" I cried, clapping my hands over my ears. Not only had my life taken a huge turn for the worse, but I had to listen to my father admit that he and his weird girlfriend did it?!

"I was hoping you'd be excited about having a brother or sister," Dad said quietly.

He looked so sad, and that made me feel really awful. Because, like I said, I wasn't excited. I had absolutely no problem with the fact that I was an only child. Who wanted to share a bathroom or fight for the remote control? And if I got bored, I could always throw a Greenie across the room and watch Miss Piggy struggle to her feet and waddle over to it. Basically, the only good thing I could see about having a brother or sister was that you had someone to blame for eating the last cookie or tracking dirt on the rug when you were too lazy to take your shoes off even though one of the house rules was "Leave your shoes near the door so you don't track dirt on the rug."

"I'm not *not* excited," I lied.

But even worse than not being excited was the fact that I was nervous. A lot of girls I knew couldn't wait to babysit, but that totally wasn't me. I had never held a baby in my entire life—what if I dropped my brother or sister? If Sarah had gotten a look at my old dolls before we gave them to Goodwill and seen how most of them were missing an arm or a leg or a head, she'd never let me hold the baby. And what about the diaper-changing thing? Marissa's aunt had let her change her baby cousin's once, and she pulled the diaper so tight around its leg that she cut off its circulation and the thing started screaming so loud that for a second Marissa said she was afraid she had gone deaf.

"I know between this news, and the fact that things with Mom and Alan are getting kind of serious, it's sort of a lot to take in, huh?" Dad said gently.

I shrugged and stared at my chana masala really, really hard so that I wouldn't start crying. Not only because I'd feel dumb, but also because I hoped to keep my makeup on for as long as possible. At least until Mom got home the next night and made me take if off. Everything was changing. And it felt like as soon as I got a handle on one thing, something else came along and pulled the rug out from under me. The divorce, being dumped, having to wear a bra, Laurel, a baby—what was next? Mom and Dad sitting me down and telling me I was adopted?

"You do know that, no matter what, we're only going to love you more, right?" he said.

I looked up at him. "But what if Mom ends up marrying Alan, and Laurel becomes my stepsister?" I blurted out. Everyone knew that babies ended up getting a lot of attention just because of the fact that they were babies and couldn't do anything, and if you didn't pay attention to them they'd literally die, but having a famous stepsister was a whole other thing.

"Well, what if she does?" he said. "Would it be so bad? You just spent fifteen minutes telling me what a good time you guys had today, even though you ended up in the security office doing it."

Yeah, we were kind-of, sort-of becoming friends, but there was no way I wanted to live with her. Even if it did mean I could borrow her makeup. "Yeah, but she's Laurel Moses," I said.

"So?"

I shook my head and made that part sigh/part grr sound that Mom made when I would say, "Fine, but just tell me why" over and over when she said I couldn't do something. Didn't he get that having her as a stepsister was a no-win situation? No matter what, I'd never measure up to her. She'd be Laurel Moses, the famous, fabulous, gorgeous star sister with the long flowy hair, and I'd be Lucy—the less pretty, untalented one with the short pixie cut. Throw a baby into the mix, and I'd be completely forgotten, like all those middle children who blend into the woodwork and are barely noticeable in family photos. At least as an only child, I couldn't be compared to anyone.

"Does Mom know about the baby?" I demanded.

Dad nodded. "We told her earlier today."

That made me feel a little better. Mom might have been acting a little crazy because she was in love, but she wasn't so crazy that she'd make me deal with a baby and a potential stepsister all at once. So at least if Mom did end up marrying Alan, it wouldn't happen until way after the baby arrived. Like two years, so I get could used to the whole thing. Because what kind of mother would want to risk her kid totally freaking out if she threw too much change at her at once. She couldn't do that.

Right?

Wrong.

At first, things seemed like they were going to be fine, because when Mom got home the following night, the first thing I did after I said, "Of course that's not smeared makeup around my eyes!" was grab her hand and look for a ring.

"What are you doing?" she asked, confused.

"Nothing," I replied, relieved, as I let her hand flop down.

Once again Marissa had been wrong. Which meant I didn't have to worry about having Laurel as a stepsister right away, and instead, all I had to worry about was dropping my new brother or sister on his or her head.

That night I finally got a good night's sleep, and by the next day it felt like things were back to normal. Well, as normal as things could possibly be when you were e-mailing and texting a major star with whom you were now kind-of, sort-of friends. We had made plans to hang out the following weekend, which was her last one in Northampton before the movie ended and she went back to New York. She had even invited me to sleep over, which was a big step, seeing that we had only just moved from archenemies to kind-of, sort-of friends. It seemed pretty soon in our friendship, but I said yes anyway. I loved staying in hotels, and Laurel had said that when she called down for room service, the chef made her stuff that wasn't even on the menu because she had posed for a picture with his daughter the week before.

And as normal as could be when you walk into your class to find everyone gathered around a computer looking at pictures of you and the famous star dressed in super-ugly outfits on WhatWereTheyThinking.com and Marissa announcing, "Personally, I think those outfits are really nice." The embarrassment of having my face splashed across the Internet again was made a little better by the fact that at least I wasn't alone in the picture—I was with a friend. Or a kind-of, sort-of friend.

Plus, having tons of people tell me how much they liked my haircut was cool. ("I can't believe Laurel Moses's own personal hairstylist cut your hair!" Marissa squealed. "Do you think if I asked really nicely he'd cut mine, too? Do you?!") Then, things started to get even better on Tuesday morning, when Rachel said hello to me. Things were on such an upswing that I was even starting to get used to the idea of having a brother or sister, as long as I wasn't asked to change his or her diaper.

And then Wednesday rolled around.

The Day It All Changed.

Mom was acting a little weird, but when wasn't she nowadays? But when I got home from riding bikes with Marissa (never that much fun, on account of the fact that she was so slow and was always stopping every two minutes to fix her helmet), she said, "Go get changed. We're going to Giovanni's for dinner." Then I started to worry. We barely ever went out to dinner on a weeknight unless it was someone's birthday. Takeout sometimes, but never an actual restaurant. The last few weeks there had been a lot of going-out-to-dinners, and none of them really turned out good for me.

"Lucy, we need to have a talk," she said after we got there and she let me order a soda, even though, like sugar, I was allowed to have it only on weekends.

My stomach dropped. Another Talk?! What were my parents trying to do to me? "About what?" I asked suspiciously.

She took a deep breath. "Well, this weekend . . . Alan asked me to marry him."

But I had checked her hand and there was no ring! I started seeing spots before my eyes. Could shock not only make your period come on but also make you go blind? "And what did you say?" I managed to get out.

"Well, I told him I needed to get your blessing before we made it official, but that if you were okay with it, my answer was yes."

Not only couldn't I see, but now I couldn't breathe as I found when I started gasping for air. This was great—all this drama was going to have me dead before I was thirteen. "What?! But you barely even know him!" I cried. "You have to know someone for at least a year before you get engaged!"

"Where'd you hear that? From Marissa?"

"No. We learned it in school," I lied. I hadn't heard it anywhere, but it sounded good. "In . . . health. Or maybe it was history. I forget."

"Lucy, honey," she said gently, "I know this has happened really fast, but sometimes that's just the way it goes. And, sure, there's always more to learn about a person, but Alan and I feel really strongly that this is it for us. That it's true love." She smiled. "In fact, I'd even go as far as to say it was love at first sight."

Now I really couldn't see. "Okay, let's say you guys did get married," I said, "and they moved into our house—" We'd have to make Mom's office in the attic into a bedroom, and I really couldn't see Laurel living there.

"They wouldn't move here. We'd move there," she said.

"Wait—what?! I can't move to New York! What about Dad? My friends? My whole life is here! They should move here—Laurel's never even in school! And when she is, she doesn't have anyone to eat lunch with!"

"But she shoots the show there—"

"So? She can just shoot it here. She's so famous I bet they'd let her do that," I said as I started crying. I felt like I had cried more in the last few months than I had in my first eleven years of life on the planet.

"Lucy, honey, it doesn't work that way. It's not just about Laurel—it's also the crew, and the production stage. I know that the idea of moving sounds really scary—I do—but if I marry Alan, unfortunately, that's the way it's got to be," she said.

In some ways it would've been easier if she was being a total jerk about it, but she wasn't—in fact, it almost looked like she was going to cry herself. Still, if she felt really bad, she wouldn't have even suggested it. I crossed my arms. "Fine—you can move. I'll stay here with Dad."

Now she looked even more hurt. "You hate the idea so much that you'd want to go live with your dad?" she said quietly.

I nodded.

"And Sarah and the baby?" she said.

Oh. Right. I had forgotten that part. That part didn't sound as good.

"For what it's worth, Laurel is really excited about the idea—" she went on.

"Wait a minute—Laurel knew about this before I did?" I cried.

"Well, yes. Alan told her last night and—"

"That's totally not fair!" I cried. "Here you are saying you want us to be a family, and then you go and leave me out right from the beginning?" It was already starting—Mom and Alan weren't even married, and already Laurel came first.

"Honey, it's not like that—"

I stood up from the table. "Yes, it is," I cried. "And you know what? I don't want to talk about this anymore!" I yelled as I ran toward the bathroom. "End of discussion!"

The only reason I came out of the bathroom was because there was a pregnant woman who really had to pee. Otherwise, I would've stayed in there all night. And before I did come out, I opened the door a crack so I could see that the pregnant woman really did exist and Mom wasn't just making that up. When we got home, I ran up to my room and locked the door, even though "No locking bedroom doors" was another house rule. I was done with house rules. Even though Mom stood at the door and said, "Lucy, please open this door so we can talk about this," and even when she came back a half hour later and said, "Lucy, your father's on the phone and he'd like to talk to you," I refused to budge. Instead, I just lay on my bed and cried. So my dad was in on this, too?! He probably couldn't wait for me to leave so he wouldn't feel so guilty giving all his attention to the baby. I couldn't believe how unfair they were being. Did they really think I'd give up my life and my friends here in Northampton just because stupid Laurel Moses had to shoot her dumb TV show? Granted other than Marissa—and as of last weekend, Laurel—I didn't really have any other friends at the moment, but that could change. (In fact, it had to change, or else I would move.)

The only time I got up was to go to the bathroom and grab Miss Piggy, who obviously knew something was really wrong because not only did she stay in my room, she let me hug her without hissing while I cried. Not even when I got her fur all wet with snot.

I was so upset that I ended up falling asleep without having dinner. And that never happened.

I refused to talk to Mom for two days. If I needed to tell her something, I used Miss Piggy to do it. Like I would say, "Miss Piggy, please ask Mom to pass the butter," or "Miss Piggy, please remind Mom that I need poster board for my book report on *A Wrinkle in Time*." I even refused to talk to Dad. The only person I talked to about it was Marissa, which, of course, was like telling the world, but I had to tell someone. When I told her, she started crying and saying, "I'M GOING TO MISS YOU SO MUCH!" over and over, even though I kept saying, "Marissa, I told you—I'm not going."

Finally, on Friday night, Mom brought home takeout from Friendly's. Probably because she felt so guilty that she was trying to ruin my life, she had gotten takeout from my favorite places the last two nights. "Okay, Lucy. You don't have to worry about it anymore," Mom said as I ate my clam roll.

"Miss Piggy," I said to the cat, who was trying to groom herself but kept falling over on account of her fatness, "please ask Mom what it is that I'm supposed to stop worrying about, because I don't know what she's talking about."

When I looked up from my clam roll, I saw that her eyes were puffy. "I had a long talk with Alan this afternoon, and I told him that we're not moving to New York."

"What do you mean?" I said. This was not what I was expecting. I was so stunned that I forgot I was supposed to go through Miss Piggy, who, at that moment, jumped up on the table and started to gobble up the fried clams that had fallen out of the roll.

"I love Alan. A lot," she said. "And I'd really like for all of us to build a life together, but you're the most important thing in the world to me. And if leaving here is going to make you so unhappy, I'm not going to do that to you."

"So you're breaking up?" I asked. It's not like I wanted that to happen. She looked so sad. I didn't want that— I just didn't want the moving/stepsister/ruining-my-life part of the whole thing.

"No. We're still going to see each other," she replied. "We'll just do the long-distance thing. Maybe at some point in the future, things will change, and you'll be open to the idea of moving, but for now we're staying here."

Okay, good. I was glad the crazy pills had worn off, finally. And, sure, not having to move was what I wanted. I had gotten my life back—or what was left of my life. I should have felt good. But I didn't—I felt guilty. "Wait— so you'd not marry him just because of me?"

"Of course," she replied. "Do you really think I'd say yes to him if you weren't one hundred percent behind the idea? I told him, we needed your blessing."

I shrugged. Marissa's mom hadn't asked her for her blessing when she married Phil.

Mom got all teary as she came around the table and hugged me. "Honey, you're my jelly bean. You're always going to come first."

Usually the "jelly-bean" thing drove me nuts—I was twelve, not six—but for some reason hearing her say it this time made me get all teary, too. It felt like she had been putting Alan and Laurel first for so long, it was good to know that she still loved me. I guess without really knowing it, I had been worried that she loved Alan more than me.

That night I slept a lot better than I had in a while. Well, at least until three, when I woke up and stared at the ceiling. Even if Alan was a worrier, and had clammy hands, and sweat when he got nervous, the truth was, when Mom was with him, her face lit up as if there were a lightbulb somewhere inside there and someone had flicked the switch to On. The only time I had seen her so happy was when she was polishing off a pint of Ben & Jerry's Chunky Monkey. And I wanted her to be happy. Because when she was happy, I was happy. Not only that, but when she was happy, I got away with things like staying up late, or having a second dessert, or getting to buy another box of maxipads.

I got up and padded into Mom's room.

"What's wrong?" she asked sleepily as I got under the covers with her.

"Nothing," I said, glad that she was wearing socks. Her feet got really cold. "I just wanted to tell you I've thought about it and ... well, I guess moving to New York wouldn't be that bad. I mean, other than the having-to-leave-my-school-and-my-friends-and-Dad part. But I guess there's a slight possibility that I'll make some new friends." Maybe. Hopefully.

She reached for the light and sat up to look me full in the face. "Really?" She looked as wide-awake as she did after her second cup of coffee.

Here was my chance to say, "Actually, no—it was a false alarm and there's no way I'm leaving here and I'm sorry to have woken you up and I'm going back to my room now." But I didn't. Instead, I shrugged and said, "Yeah. I mean, as long as I can come back and visit a lot."

"Oh Lucy!" she said, covering my face with kisses. "Of course you can!"

"Mom, Mom, it's okay," I said, trying to wiggle away. I loved my mother, but man, did she have bad breath in the middle of the night. According to Dr. Kantor, my dentist, it's because when you sleep with your mouth open like she does, bacteria gets in and causes the smell.

After she settled down, we closed our eyes. I never slept in the same bed with her anymore, unless I fell asleep watching a movie or something, but I knew that once we moved, I wouldn't be able to do it even if I wanted to, so I figured I might as well do it one last time.

I sure hoped I wasn't making a huge mistake, Because the thought of packing up my room, and then unpacking in New York, and then packing up again to come back to Northampton sounded really tiring.

I didn't even have to wait until I got to New York to realize I had made a huge mistake—I found out when we had breakfast with Alan and Laurel the next morning.

My first clue should have been when, after we sat down, instead of Laurel being all excited like Mom had said she was and saying something like,"I'm so glad you changed your mind and we're going to be stepsisters!" she basically ignored me and barely said a word to me other than a very unfriendly "Hi" in response to my

"Hey." She didn't even take off her sunglasses, which was not only very movie star–like, but also rude.

"So I guess that stuff about Things Getting Serious was true," I said as Mom and Alan looked at the menu and marveled over the fact it wasn't until just then that they realized they had another thing in common—that they both liked their eggs scrambled. "We're going to be sisters, huh?"

She took off her sunglasses and looked at me. "Stepsisters," she corrected, coldly. Why were her eyes puffy? Had she been crying?

I waited for a smile or an "I'm just kidding" or something like that, but there was nothing.

Wait a minute—what was going on? What happened to the Laurel's-really-excited-about-the-idea part? If anyone should have been cold and mean, it was me. It's not like she was the one being uprooted from the only place she'd ever lived, and all of her friends, and her dad—I was.

If that wasn't a big enough clue that something was wrong, there was the fact that as we started what Alan called "our first official meal as a family" ("We're not a family yet," I corrected him, which earned me a "Lucy" in one of Mom's warning tones), I found out we were moving in SIX WEEKS.

I was so shocked I just let the syrup I was pouring on my pancakes keep going to the point where I ruined them. Too much syrup was just as bad as not enough syrup. "But ... What about school? I was thinking we'd move, like, when the school year was over," I sputtered. Sure, no matter when I got there I'd still be known as the New Girl, but my feeling was that with everyone having to remember new locker combinations and schedules, it would make it so that there was less attention on me and I could hopefully blend in easier.

"You didn't tell her about the couple from Boston?" Alan asked.

"What couple from Boston?" I demanded.

It turned out that Mom had talked to a Realtor about putting the house up for sale. And this was before I had even said I'd go ("I was just trying to be prepared in case you changed your mind, honey! And, look, it worked!"). There was a couple from Boston who was willing to pay full price for our house, as long as they could have it right away.

What else had been going on behind my back? If it turned out Mom was pregnant, too, I'd just die. I didn't really think she was, because once when I was overlistening to her and Deanna talk, she said that, because she was forty-seven, "The store was officially closed," whatever that meant. But who knew anymore?

Alan turned to Mom. "We should go check in with the Realtor and see if there's any news. We can let the girls do some pre–family bonding!"

Ha. As if I was interested in doing any of that at the moment.

"I know we talked about you sleeping over tonight,"

Laurel said coldly, "but suddenly I don't feel all that well."

"Fine," I snapped. "Because I don't feel well either." That wasn't a lie—I felt sick to my stomach.

What had I gotten myself into?

Six weeks goes really fast when you have to pack up your entire life and say good-bye to every person, place, and thing that you've ever known. Especially if you're not a good packer to begin with. Every time I came across something, I ended up wasting a lot of time sitting there thinking about all the memories that go along with it. Not only that, but there was the this-is-the-last-time-I'll-ever . . . game to play. This is the last red velvet cupcake I'll ever have from Sweet Lady Jane. (Well, until I came back to visit.) This is the last time I'll have to take a pop quiz on mixed fractions. (I was seriously hoping they didn't have them in New York.) This is the last time I'll have to feel like a complete loser as Rachel and Missy whisper and giggle over all the private jokes that I'm not a part of now. (Although Rachel had said hello that one time, nothing had happened after that. I would've thought once they heard I was moving, they would've been nice, but nope.)

When I wasn't packing, or eating all my favorite things for the last time or the second-to-last-time or the third-to-last-time, I was hanging out with Dad. Although he said he'd miss me, he said he was excited for me to have such a big adventure. At first I thought he was just saying that to be nice and in truth he wouldn't miss me—that, actually, he was relieved because it meant he wouldn't feel so guilty for spending time with the baby. But then one night when we were playing Monopoly, I looked up and saw a tear sliding down his face, which made me happy and sad and embarrassed at the same time.

Finally, after one last pizza at Frankie's with him and Sarah, it was moving day. After I had taken one last walk through my house and said good-bye to every room (I even said it out loud, which probably sounded weird, but I didn't care), I went outside. Dad and Sarah and Marissa were waiting.

"Here," Sarah said, holding out a little glass bottle. "This lavender essential oil will help with the anxiety of the move," she said.

"Thanks," I said, giving her a hug. I patted her stomach, which, because she was only three months pregnant, wasn't very big. Dad called it a "food baby." "Take care of my brother or sister," I said.

She smiled. "I will. I can't wait until you can come back and babysit."

I wanted to say, "Um, I'm not so sure that's a good idea," but I didn't. Instead, I gave a semi-fake smile and said, "Oh boy, I can't wait!"

Next to her, Marissa was crying. "Omigod, I can't

believe my best friend in the entire world is LEAVING!" she wailed. "I'm going to miss you sooooo much!"

"You'll be okay, Marissa," I said. I reached into my knapsack. "Here—I thought you should have this," I said, handing her the purple notebook.

She gasped. "You're making me Keeper of the Periods?"

I shrugged. "Well, someone's got to do it."

This made her cry even more. "Omigod—this is the nicest thing anyone's ever done for me in my entire life!" she wailed as she threw her arms around my neck.

Okay, so maybe there were some things I wouldn't miss. "But the only thing is—when I get mine, I need you to write it in there. Even if I don't live here anymore, it's only fair."

"Totally! I promise. I'll even use my silver glitter pen. So when can I come visit you?" she demanded.

"Ummm...I don't know yet. I'll e-mail you," I replied, trying to pull away.

"I'm going to miss you soooooooo much," she cried.

"I know. You already said that."

She looked at her watch. "Wow—I didn't realize it was so late! I have to get home. Now that you're leaving, I told Brianna we could be BFFs, so we're going to the mall. See ya!" she said as she sprinted away.

She was so...Marissa.

At last, I got to Dad. Please don't cry, please don't cry, I said to myself. I didn't just mean him—I meant me, too.

"Bye, Dad," I said as a huge tear fell and plopped right in the middle of my chest.

"Bye, monkey," he said, smothering me in a hug, his own tears falling on my head. "You're going to be just fine."

"I am?" I whispered.

"Uh-huh," he promised.

"Okay," I said. I tried to undo myself from the hug, but he just hugged tighter. "Uh, Dad? You can let go now."

"Sorry," he said, releasing me.

Finally, Alan, Mom, and I got in the car along with a yowling Miss Piggy. Because she meowed at the top of her lungs during the five-minute drive to the vet, I didn't even want to think of the headache I'd have after five hours.

I stared out the back window until I couldn't see them anymore. I turned around and gave a big sigh.

I could always move back if New York turned out to be really bad.

Right?

chapter 11

Dear Dr. Maude,

Okay, I know on your website you say you're a "die-hard New Yorker," and I know there are all these commercials that play in the back of taxicabs about how it's the best city in the world, but even though I've only been here two days and Mom says I have to give it time, I just don't get why anyone would live here. Not only is it loud, and people don't even say "I'm sorry" when they bump into you, but cars try and mow you over when you're crossing the street even when the walk sign is lit up! That's when you're SUPPOSED to be crossing.

School doesn't start for another week (it's spring break here), but I don't even know if I'll still be ALIVE by then. Which, to be honest, might not be a bad thing, because from the pictures I saw in the Center for Creative Learning brochure, those kids look REALLY stuck-up. The only good news is that Laurel is shooting a movie in L.A., so I still have a few more days before she's home and I start feeling completely unwanted, which is how she made me feel the few other times I saw her after that awful breakfast the morning I told Mom I'd move.

Dr. Maude, it's completely obvious that moving here was a HUGE mistake. So what do I do now????

I wish I knew where you lived because if I did, maybe we could talk about this in person rather than through e-mail. Well, that is, if you ever write me back.

yours truly,
Lucy B. Parker

Mom says that sometimes I tend to exaggerate, but I totally wasn't exaggerating when it came to New York being a very unfriendly place to live. From the very first time I got into the elevator by myself at the Conran—the apartment building that Alan and Laurel live in (Mom keeps trying to correct me by saying it's our building now, too, but I'm sorry, this place will never be home for me)—I knew I was in trouble.

After we arrived, Alan showed us around the apartment, which took a while because it was humungous. Unlike Dad's apartment, which had two bedrooms, their apartment had four, which was as big as our house in Northampton. Sorry—our EX-house. And unlike our ex-house, there was no creaking when you stepped on the hardwood floors, and all of their windows or doors shut right, because they weren't over a hundred years old. It was the penthouse apartment, which meant that it was on the very top floor of the building—the twenty-first floor—which was so high, my ears popped in the elevator. Everything looked completely brand-new, even though Laurel and Alan had lived there for four years. Brand-new and super-, super-clean. Well, at least until Miss Piggy threw up a hairball right in the center of the living room rug fifteen minutes after we arrived.

There were no dust bunnies in the corners, and everything in the kitchen gleamed. But we didn't get to meet Rose, the housekeeper/nanny who had been with Alan and Laurel since right after Laurel's mother died, because it was her day off and she was at church. Even though Laurel was in L.A. (usually Alan would've been there with her, but because (a) it was only a week's shoot and (b) we were moving in, her assistant was acting as her guardian), it felt like she was there. Everywhere you looked there were pictures of her. Some were just regular framed pictures, but then there were also pictures of her with other famous people and framed posters of the movies she was in. As Alan gave us the tour, I started to get really nervous that it was only a matter of time before I broke something, like the television in the living room that was so big it looked like a movie-theater screen. My coordination problem was not going to make living here easy.

"And this is your bedroom, Lucy," Alan said as we walked into a plain white room that was almost one and a half times bigger than my old one. I guess part of why it looked so big was that, other than a bed and a dresser, there was nothing else in it. Mom had decided that our furniture wouldn't look right in the apartment, so we sold it all on Craigslist before we moved. (Except for the really ugly stuff—that we gave to Goodwill.) At first I was really upset, but now, after seeing the place, I realized she was right. Plus, she told me I could pick out anything I wanted for my bedroom. "Laurel had been using it as her workout room, which is why it's so bare bones at the moment," Alan explained. I was glad to find that it was pretty much the same size as Laurel's bedroom, because if hers was a lot bigger than mine, I was going to have to take Mom aside and say something to her, because that totally wouldn't be fair.

"And I can decorate it any way I want, right?" I asked.

"Yes. Within reason," Mom warned, probably thinking about the time a few years ago when I asked her if we could hire her artist friend Sierra to paint a mural of the African jungle on one of my walls.

When I opened the closet door, I felt like I had hit the jackpot. I never had to worry about cleaning up again—it was huge! I could shove everything I owned in there and still have room for more. "Can I paint it purple?" I asked.

"Purple?" Alan asked. "Uh, I guess...," he said nervously, "but wouldn't you rather have a nice neutral color...like that pretty beige that Laurel has in her room?"

What I wanted to say was, "You mean that color that's so boring it's not even color?" But instead, I just shrugged. It was starting already. This was exactly what happened when Marissa's mom married Phil—this I'm-going-to-pretend-to-be-really-nice-to-you-but-really-we're-going-to-do-it-all-MY-way thing.

Alan glanced over at Mom for support. I couldn't be sure, but it seemed to me that Mom gave him one of her looks—in this case, the one that meant "Please just be the bigger person here, okay?"

"On second thought, I think purple would look great in here," he said.

Score one for Lucy B. Parker.

By the time I went to bed that night, my brain felt like it was going to burst from all the instructions Alan had thrown at me. Stuff like "To turn the TV on, you use this remote...but if you're going to be watching a DVD, you use this remote" and "This is the keypad for the alarm. Now, when you leave, you punch in 7-7-2-8-0. But when you come back, you punch in 5-4-2-8-4" and "If you're ever taking a cab home, you tell the guy you're going to 158 Central Park West, which is between Seventy-sixth and Seventy-seventh."

Who could remember all these numbers?!

Right before I went to bed I called Dad, in hopes that he could just cheer me up a little, but all I got was his voice mail. I was so desperate to talk to someone from Northampton that I called Marissa, but even she wasn't around because she was sleeping over at Brianna's.

I wasn't even gone twenty-four hours and it was like already everyone had forgotten about me and moved on.

The next afternoon, we went out for lunch (from the number of restaurants we passed and the crowds of people waiting to get in, it seemed like all people in New York did was eat), and Alan gave Mom and me a tour of the neighborhood. ("This is Central Park. This is the Museum of Natural History. This is the homeless guy who's been standing at this same corner screaming about how the world is going to end for the last five years.") We were walking back to the apartment when Alan told me he had a surprise for me.

"What is it?" I asked warily. Frankly, over the last few months, I had had enough surprises to last me for my entire life.

"You'll see, you'll see," he said excitedly as he pressed the 10 button when we got in the elevator instead of 21.

When we got off, he led Mom and me to 10D and buzzed the buzzer. The hideous noise that was coming from inside the apartment stopped, and a minute later a short girl around my age with a dark bob, pale skin, and a big nose answered the door.

"Can I help you?" she asked politely. Like a lot of people I had seen on the streets during our walk around the neighborhood, she was dressed all in black. In her case, black jeans and a black sweater. The only color

I could see were the electric blue–painted toenails on her bare feet. Those were actually pretty cool.

"Are you Beatrice?" Alan asked.

"Yes, but I prefer the Italian pronunciation—Bay-a-tree-chay," she replied. Politely, again. Everyone said that New Yorkers were so rude, but this girl was anything but. I wondered if she was one of those kids who just acted like this in front of adults, but when you got her alone she was normal. For her sake, I hoped so—otherwise, I bet she didn't have a lot of friends.

"Oh. Well, it's very nice to meet you, Beatrice," Alan said, pronouncing it her way. "I'm Alan Moses, from 21C. I ran into your mom in the lobby the other day, and she told me that you're a sixth grader at the Center for Creative Learning—"

Oh no, I thought, immediately ducking behind Mom. I knew exactly what Alan was doing—he was trying to make a friend for me. I hated when adults did that. I was twelve, not four. I didn't need playdates arranged for me.

Hiding behind Mom didn't work. Alan grabbed my arm and pulled me forward so I was face-to-face with the girl with the weird name. Except she was so short it was more like she was eye level with my boobs.

"And amazingly enough, Lucy here is going to be joining your class once spring break is over! I mean, what are the odds that in a city of eight million people and so many private schools, two girls living in the same building would end up in the same class!"

Could Alan be more embarrassing? I wanted to sink into the floor and melt away.

"So I wanted to introduce you two so you could start to become friends," he continued. "Lucy just moved here yesterday from Massachusetts, and she doesn't know any other girls other than my daughter, who's out of town at the moment, so I know she'd appreciate it if you could maybe give her the lowdown on the Center. I was thinking maybe the two of you could hang out this week. Maybe do a little shopping."

Yup, it turned out he could be more embarrassing. I turned to Mom with a um-can-you-please-help-me-out-here? look, but she appeared just as excited as Alan was about the idea of this girl and me becoming friends.

"Oh," the girl said, stepping back. "Well, I'd like to, but I have a lot of studying to do this coming week." She gave me a small smile. "Welcome to Manhattan, Lucy," she said politely. "I'll see you in school. Maybe we can do something at a later time. It was very nice meeting all of you, but if you'll excuse me, I have to get back to practicing the piano," she said as she closed the door.

So that's what that hideous noise was. But while it made me feel a little bit better to know that there was someone on this planet who seemed to be as uncoordinated as me, it didn't feel so good that that someone seemed to have no interest in becoming friends with me. I mean, it's not like I really wanted to be friends with her anyway, especially not after Alan had embarrassed me like that. And we seemed like total opposites anyway—her, all in black with no color, while I had on my tie-dyed Converses and rainbow suspenders. But, still, when someone would rather study over vacation than hang out with you, it kind of makes you feel like a total loser.

I realized the next day that moving makes you really tired. Not so much the unpacking part—which is pretty easy, for someone like me, who thinks that just dumping everything in drawers and the closet is a perfectly fine way to organize things—but the part where it takes you twice as long to do something because up until two days before you had lived in the same house for your entire life and now it's all so new. Like, say, figuring out how to turn the shower on or needing to open up every drawer in the kitchen before finally getting to the one with the silverware. After lunch I asked Mom if I could walk down to the bodega (according to Alan, it's the Spanish word for 7-Eleven) to get a soda so I would have more energy to keep unpacking/shoving stuff in the closet. She tried to convince me to wait until she figured out how to use the super-fancy washing machine and then she'd go with me so I didn't get lost. I blew up at her and went on about how I wasn't a baby, and how lost could a person get when all the streets were numbered, and that seeing that she had made me leave my home, the least she could do was let me take a walk by myself down the block. Then I added that if she thought she was going to be walking me to school every day, she was in for a big surprise.

After I was done I felt bad, and was about to apologize, but before I could, she got all teary and smothered me in a hug and said, "Ohhh . . . your hormones are really kicking into gear!" She said that whenever I got snippy with her nowadays, which was beyond annoying. "But you're absolutely right—you're not a baby anymore. Obviously," she added as she pointed to my chest. "You're a beautiful young woman. I do have to learn to let you separate from me, so, yes," she said, reaching into her purse for a five-dollar bill, "you can go to the bodega by yourself. Right after you go put your bra on."

I was relieved to get away for a while, even if I had to wear a bra to do it, except for the fact that it meant even more directions to remember ("Okay, now when you get out of the building, you're going to turn right on Central Park West," Alan explained. "And then you're going to turn right again on Seventy-sixth Street. And then you're going to pass Amsterdam until you get to Columbus, and the bodega will be on your left-hand side."). When he asked if I wanted him to write it all down for me, I almost went off on him like I had on Mom, but instead, I just said very politely, "No, thank you. I'll be fine," because (a) I didn't feel comfortable enough with him yet to yell at him and (b) knowing how nervous he got, I was afraid he'd start to cry or something.

Unfortunately, Mom was right, I wasn't very good with directions (I blame that whole uncoordination thing). The minute I walked out of the apartment, I turned left to go to the elevator instead of right. Once I did get in, it stopped at the seventeenth floor, and an older woman wearing a fur coat got on with one of those yippy little shih tzu dogs. Because the Conran was such a fancy building on one of the nicest streets in New York (literally across the street from Central Park), I had a feeling that the woman's coat was definitely real fur rather than fake, but from the scowl on her face, I didn't think me saying, "You know, some baby animal died just so you could wear that coat," was a friendly neighbor thing to say. So instead, I said, "Hi—my name is Lucy B. Parker, and I just moved into the building. 21C. I like your dog's sweater." Usually, I think dogs that wear sweaters look really stupid, but in this case I wasn't lying—the sweater was really cute. It was leopard print, and it paired well with the dog's rhinestone collar.

Instead of saying something like, "Nice to meet you, Lucy. Welcome to the neighborhood, and that was really nice of you to compliment my dog's sweater," the lady didn't even bother to look away from the elevator numbers as she said, "Hmph." In Northampton, when someone new moved into the neighborhood, people brought them cookies, and sometimes—if you were Mrs. Moore—even an entire apple cobbler. Here at the Conran, it was like one of the rules of the building was

"Please make sure to be as unfriendly as possible to your neighbors."

After that I didn't try to make any more small talk. Instead, I spent the rest of the ride swallowing so that my ears would stop popping and I didn't go deaf. In the lobby, Pepe, the old doorman who wore a hearing aid, gave me a look like he had no idea who I was when I said hello to him, even though Alan kept introducing me to him every time we saw him. Outside, I turned left instead of right, and went up Seventy-seventh Street instead of Seventy-sixth. Then, when I got to Columbus, there was no bodega, so I kept walking to Broadway. The only bodega-looking thing was across the street, but I almost got hit by a car trying to cross, even though I had the WALK sign.

After I got my soda and a Blow Pop, I headed back to the apartment. But I had already walked three blocks before I realized that I was going the wrong way and was at Eightieth Street. Then, when I turned around and started going the right way, some lady who totally wasn't looking where she was going because she was too busy checking her e-mail on her BlackBerry banged straight into me, and my soda went flying all over the new Angry Little Girls! T-shirt that Dad had gotten me as a going-away present. She didn't say sorry or anything. I had some money left over, but there was no way I was going to try to retrace my steps back to the bodega, because I was afraid I'd end up in New Jersey or something.

I knew by this time Mom was probably totally freaking out because it had been, like, fifteen minutes since I left. And even though I had sworn to her that I was just going to the bodega and back (which Alan said would take approximately seven minutes—ten, maybe, if I spend a lot of time going over my soda choices), she probably figured I'd gotten lost and run over by a truck or something. I reached into my pocket for my cell phone and realized I had left it on my bed. Oops.

When I got back to the Conran, I was thirsty, sticky, and *thisclose* to crying. It had been fewer than three days since I had been gone from Northampton, but I missed everything about it. I hated not knowing my way around, and I had no idea how I was going to get through the next six years until I left for college. Then, as if things weren't bad enough, as I tried to walk into the building, some guy wearing the same doorman uniform as Pepe but who was not Pepe barked, "Excuse me—can I help you with something, miss?" While Pepe couldn't hear and had no memory and probably couldn't have stopped someone from going in if he tried, this guy was tall, with jet black hair and muscles, and, because he was frowning, he looked pretty scary.

"I'm just going up to"—"my apartment" didn't sound right because it really wasn't my apartment, it was Laurel and Alan's apartment, and I had a feeling that, no matter what, it was never, ever going to feel like mine—"the place where I'm living," I said nervously.

"And that would be where?" the guy demanded.

"Apartment 21C."

He blocked the door. "Nice try. Now it's time to leave."

"Huh?" I said, confused. Wow. Even the doormen in New York were unfriendly.

"Look, you want a signed picture or something, you can go to LaurelMoses.com, and there's directions there about how to do that," he said, "but if you don't leave right now, I'm gonna have to call the police." He looked me up and down. "You look like a nice girl—don't go ruining your life by getting arrested for stalking and sent to juvenile hall. Something like that could keep you out of college."

This was just the last straw. Even though it was completely embarrassing, I couldn't help myself and started to cry. "Wait a minute—you think I'm stalking Laurel Moses?!" I cried. "I am so not! The only reason I'm here is because my mother is marrying Laurel Moses's father, which meant we had to move here because of her…television show"—I almost said "stupid television show," but for all I knew, this man was also a huge Laurel Moses fan and loved her dumb music. I started to cry even harder. "Believe me, if it were up to me, I wouldn't be going up to 21C—I'd be going to 42 Massasoit Street in Northampton, Massachusetts!"

"Ohhhh," the mean guy said, reaching inside his jacket pocket and handing me not a regular tissue but a fancy cloth handkerchief. "So you're Lucy!" he said. "I'm sorry. My bad. I didn't think you were coming until next weekend."

"You know my name?" I sniffled into the handkerchief.

"Sure. Alan's been talking about you and your mom nonstop. And that guy can talk, if you know what I mean," he said with a wink. He held out his hand. "I'm Pete. Your new doorman."

I honked into the handkerchief and held out my hand. "Lucy B. Parker," I said. I had to say, the idea of having my own personal doorman did sound kind of cool.

"Sorry about what just happened, but you can never be too careful," he said. "You wouldn't believe some of the stuff people have tried to pull over the years to try and get near Laurel."

"Like what?" I sniffled.

"Oh, lots of things," he replied. "Showing up dressed up in a bear outfit with balloons to sing 'Happy Birthday,' even though Laurel's birthday wasn't for another four months. Long-lost cousins. That kind of stuff. So *qué pasa*, girl? You look a little upset there. I mean, even before I laid into you." He pointed to the couch inside the lobby. "Cop a squat and tell Pete what's goin' on."

I don't know what it was about him—maybe it was because he was the only person in New York who had been nice to me so far, or maybe it was just because I was so lonely—but I did what he said. I told him about Mom meeting Alan, and how at first I said I didn't want to move, but then I said I would, and how now I was worried that I had made the wrong decision, and that I was scared to start school the following week because what if no one wanted to be friends with the New Girl, and what was I going to do when it came time to figuring where to sit at lunch, and how was I going to find my way around the city without getting lost, and what was I going to do when Laurel got back from L.A., because the last time I had seen her she was as excited about the whole stepsister thing as I was—which is to say, not very.

Pete didn't say much as I went on and on. Instead, he just stroked his chin, although at certain points he did say, "Mmm," and "Uh-huh, uh-huh," and "I see." When I was done, he stroked his chin some more. "Okay, so you didn't ask or anything, but if I may, can I give you some advice?" he said.

I nodded.

"Now I understand that all this is a big change and all, but as far as I can see, the solution's pretty simple."

"What is it?" I asked, leaning in to make sure I wouldn't miss what came next. Since Dr. Maude wasn't e-mailing me back, I'd take advice wherever I could get it.

"Just be yourself." He shrugged.

"And what else?" I said.

"What d'you mean, 'what else'?" he replied. "That's it. Can't go wrong with that. See, if you're yourself, then you're gonna meet the people you're supposed to meet, and become friends with the people you're supposed to be friends with. Now, I don't know you all that well, Lucy, but I can tell you this—I am very good judge of character. You have to be when you're a doorman. And just from the short time we've known each other, I can already tell that you're a very special young lady and you're gonna do just great here in New York City and make lots of friends. So don't worry about it, okay?" He reached into his pocket. "Now, you like Sour Patch Kids by any chance?"

I nodded. "They're my favorite candy."

"Good. Mine, too," he said as he took out a box and shook some out into my hand. "I knew there was a reason I liked you right away. It's all going to be okay, I promise. I'm a doorman—we know these things."

Boy, I hoped he was right. Pete may not have been Dr. Maude, but he seemed pretty sure of what he was talking about.

chapter 12

Dear Dr. Maude,

Well, the good news is I made my first friend in New York. His name is Pete. The bad news is, he's forty-nine years old and my doorman, so it's not exactly like he's someone I can go to H&M with. He's really nice, though. Yesterday when I came back from my walk (I'm proud to say that this time I got only a little instead of a lot lost) and gave him the cupcake I had bought him (I will admit that the two cupcakes I've had since I've been here in New York City have been very good), he was so touched he actually started to cry. According to him, Puerto Ricans (which is what he is, even though he grew up in East Harlem rather than in Puerto Rico) are very passionate people. So I guess even if a lot of the people who live here in the Conran are stuck-up because, according to Pete, Central Park West is one of the fanciest streets in all of Manhattan, at least I have him.

Unfortunately, I can't have him with me all the time, like, say, tonight, when Laurel comes back from L.A. and we have our first family dinner, or tomorrow, when I have my first day of school. I'm REALLY, REALLY nervous about all of this. So nervous that, other than the cupcake, I've barely eaten anything all day. And that never happens to me.

Pete says I just need to be myself and everything will work out just fine, but I don't know if I believe that. Do you think that's enough? Or is there more I have to do?

If there is more I have to do, when you write back, do you think you could explain it with as few directions as possible? Because my brain feels like it's going to explode from everything I have to remember nowadays.

yours truly,
LUCY B. PARKER

P.S. Not like I would ever stalk you or anything, but do you think when you write back you could also tell me what part of the city you live in, just so when I think about you reading this, I can picture where you might be? For instance, yesterday Alan took us to the Upper East Side, so now I know what that looks like. And the day before that we went down to Greenwich Village, so I know what that looks like, too. If I find out you live on the Upper West Side like I do, I'll just die!

Okay, that just-be-the-bigger-person-because-it'll-give-you-good-karma thing that Dad is always telling me to do?

Total waste of time.

Because after Mom and I got back from H&M (one good thing about moving=three new outfits for school), I spent the entire afternoon NOT doing stuff for myself and my first day of school—like, say, practicing getting my hair just right with the mousse and gel Mom had bought me—and instead being the bigger person and focusing on Laurel coming home. First, after finding my way home after ending up all the way over at Riverside Park instead of Central Park when I got lost on my way back from the art supply store, I made this really cool WELCOME HOME, LAUREL!!! sign—complete with glitter—and hung it above her bed, and then I blew up balloons and hung streamers. After that, Rose—who had become my second friend in New York after she found out that I liked *telenovelas*, too, which are soap operas in Spanish, even though I couldn't understand a word of them—helped me bake a Welcome Home carrot cake. Other than the fact that it was a little lopsided and had a finger dent on the side from where I swiped some icing, it looked very professional.

If anyone should have gone out of her way to be the nice and welcoming one, it was technically Laurel, since she didn't have to give up her whole life to be there. But I figured that if I was the bigger person and did it first, maybe she'd suddenly be happy that I had moved into her house and I could get a good night's sleep so I didn't show up at my first day of school with dark circles under my eyes.

Yeah, if, after being on a plane for six hours, I was pounced on by paparazzi shoving cameras in my face as I made my way to my car, and then, after that, if

I had to go in the back entrance of my building because there were so many photographers camped out in front, I'd probably be cranky, too. But even if I were cranky because of all that, when I walked into my room and saw how someone had taken the time to decorate it with balloons, streamers, a sign, and confetti on my bed, I'd throw my arms around the decorator and say, "Holy moly—this is amazing! I'm so lucky to have such a thoughtful stepsister-to-be!" instead of just standing there like a lump and saying, "Oh. Wow."

"Do you like it?" I asked anxiously. I was especially proud of how well the bubble letters in the sign had turned out. Because of the coordination thing, anything art-related is also a problem for me, too.

"Oh, it's great," she said, walking over to one of the streamers. For an actress, she didn't sound all that convincing. "It's just . . . did you use tape to put this stuff up?"

I nodded. Of course. What did she think I used—glue?

She carefully lifted the corner of the streamer off the wall and peered at the wall. "Tape can peel the paint off, though."

What? Here I was, trying to do something nice, and instead I was getting accused of ruining her walls.

"I mean, it was super-sweet of you to do this," she said as she started to take the streamer off. "But if you don't mind, I'm going to take it down because they just repainted the walls a month ago." She walked over to the sign and took that down, too. "I'm totally going to prop the sign up in the corner, though, because it's really beautiful. I love the glitter." She picked up one of her pillows and brushed the confetti off. "A person could choke on this confetti, though."

"Sorry to make such a mess of your room," I mumbled before walking out. Here I was just trying to get closer to Laurel, and instead I felt like a total screwup. Like any minute I was going to be arrested for breaking and entering and attempted murder.

I didn't exactly ignore Laurel for the rest of the evening, but I sure didn't go out of my way to be extra nice to her, and she did the same. It was kind of like when you've had a fight with a person but neither of you want to acknowledge that you've had a fight, so you're talking but you're not really talking, if that makes sense.

We had just finished our first official Parker-Moses Family Dinner of Chinese food from a place called Shun Lee (it's supposed to be one of the best restaurants in the city, but, as far as I was concerned, it wasn't half as good as Madame Wu's) when Alan dinged his glass with his knife. I still couldn't get used to how all the dishes and glasses in their apartment matched. Back home, a lot of our stuff had come from flea markets and thrift stores because of Mom's it's-so-much-better-to-have-stuff-with-character-and-history thing. Obviously we washed it really well before using it. But before we moved, she sold most of it back to a consignment shop, so now, instead of drinking my iced tea out of my favorite VIRGINIA IS FOR LOVERS glass that we had found at the Pioneer Valley Flea Market one Sunday afternoon, I was using a plain-glass glass. Which matched the other plain-glass glasses on the table. And instead of my Chinese food being on my favorite chipped blue-and-white-checked plate, it was on an unchipped plain white plate, which was just like the other unchipped plain white plates on the table.

"Okay, folks, it's now time for the first official Parker-Moses family meeting," Alan announced. He reached for the little notebook and pen he carried everywhere. "Lucy, would you like to be the one to take the notes?"

I gave Mom a look. But she seemed just as confused as me. We never had official family meetings back in Northampton. Instead, our family meetings took place with me yelling through the bathroom door while Mom peed.

"Uh, okay," I replied. I did have good penmanship. Maybe my letters weren't as bubbly as Laurel's, but they were still neat.

"So is there any old business anyone would like to bring up?" he asked.

"How can there be old business if this is the first meeting?" Laurel asked.

"Good point," he replied. "Okay, so moving on to new business." He reached for four copies of a bunch of typed pages stapled together and handed them out to us.

"Honey, what's this?" Mom asked, in the same worried tone she used when, back when I was seven, the sea monkeys I had sent away for using my birthday money from my grandmother had arrived.

"Well, I took the liberty of putting together what I thought would be some helpful guidelines," he replied.

"One: The choice for what to watch during family TV hour will rotate weekly so each member will get to choose once a month," Mom read aloud. "Two: A list of possible topics of conversation for family dinners will be presented to Alan fifteen minutes before said family dinner so he can prepare an agenda . . . Three: No going to bed angry with another family member."

Okay, we had had the "No going to bed angry" rule in the Parker house, too, but an agenda for dinner conversation? These other ones made it sound like I was at military school like Frankie Bankuti's brother.

"Ah, honey?" Mom said.

"Yes, angel?" Alan replied.

"Can we discuss this later?" she asked, motioning to the guidelines.

"Is something wrong?" he asked anxiously.

"Well . . . all of this just feels very . . . structured."

"Dad and I have always been really structured," Laurel piped up. "My therapist says the more unstructured time

183

a person has, the more anxious she gets." I wondered if she was going to tell her therapist about how I had almost ruined her walls. Or how she had changed her mind and now wished she hadn't said yes when her father had brought up the idea of marrying my mother.

Mom and I looked at each other, and the panicky feeling that had been in the bottom of my stomach since we had arrived started moving up into my chest.

All these rules. All these directions. Matching dishes. A soon-to-be-stepsister who thought I was trying to kill her with confetti. A new school. I wondered if it was too late to change my mind and ask Mom if we could move back. At Target, as long as you had your receipt, you had thirty days to return something, and we'd been in New York City only eight days.

"Lucy?" Laurel said later as I was eating my second slice of carrot cake in the kitchen. There was a lot left on account of the fact that it turned out I had read the directions wrong and told Rose it had to bake for only thirty-five instead of forty-five minutes, so when we cut into it, it was really mushy. Personally, I liked cakes that were sort of raw because it made them more moist, but no one else seemed to feel the same way.

"Yeah?" I was starting to feel a little nauseous, though, but I couldn't tell if it was from the cake or the fact that in twelve hours I'd be at my new school.

"When you're done watching TV, you have to push the button on the clicker twice, or else the TV doesn't turn off and it stays lit up even though you can't see the picture, so it wastes electricity," she said. "And we always put the remote in the drawer underneath the TV so we can find it easily."

"Oh. Sorry," I said. Back in Northampton, our remote usually ended up underneath the sofa cushion.

"That's okay," she replied with her fake smile. "I just wanted to tell you, you know, for future reference." Maybe it was my imagination, but I felt like she was looking at me like my grandmother used to look at Daisy, her dog, before she was housetrained and kept peeing on the rug. "Well, good night."

"Good night," I replied. I wanted to say, "Make sure you do a confetti check before you turn out the light," but I didn't.

"Lucy?" she said the next morning as I was in my bathroom trying to copy what I had read in her *Teen Vogue* the week before about how to make my hair look just the exact right amount of messed-up with my new gel.

"Yeah?"

She held up the magazine. "I don't mind if you borrow my magazines, but do you think you could make sure not to put anything on them? It looks like you put a water glass on the cover and it left a ring," she said.

"Oh. Sorry about that," I said, feeling dumb again. I felt like the only thing I had said to her since she had gotten home was "Sorry."

"And when you're done, if you could put them back in the magazine rack with the fashion magazines, that would be great."

"I did."

"Actually, you didn't. It was with the news magazines."

Who had separate magazine racks for news magazines and fashion magazines? I hadn't known I was moving into a library. Next thing you knew she'd have me alphabetizing my books.

"Well … I hope you have a good first day at school," she said. "Your hair looks really cute, by the way."

"It does?"

She nodded.

"Thanks," I said. See, that was more the kind of thing I had been hoping to hear from a stepsister-to-be. "Your hair looks cute … do you want to go get manicures together?"— that kind of thing. Not, "Please don't ruin my walls with tape and why do you have to be so messy?" I opened my mouth to say, "Hey, so do you want to maybe hang out after I get home from school and you get home from the studio?" but she was gone before I could get the words out.

"I've just never met someone so … clean," I said to Rose as I ate the homemade fried plantains she had brought

186

me from her apartment in Brooklyn. Because plantains are bananas, which are a fruit, I figured they were okay to eat as a breakfast food, even if there was a ton of brown sugar and honey on them. But, still, I was glad Mom and Alan were on their morning jog (another thing they had in common! Ugh) and weren't around to see it.

Rose laughed her great laugh, which came all the way from deep in her belly. "Oh baby, you have no idea how clean that child is!" she boomed in her Jamaican accent. "One time after I dusted her room, I walked by ten minutes later and she was dusting it all over again!" She shook her head and sighed. "And the way she goes into her closet and makes sure there's equal amounts of space into between her clothes." She shook her head. "People have all sorts of ways to pretend they in charge of the world and not God."

"What do you mean?" I asked.

"She doesn't do that stuff just to be fussy and make you feel bad, baby," Rose explained. "She does it because her life is so crazy. People are always snapping her picture and acting like they know her. That's a lot for a little girl to handle, even if she makes almost as much money as the Oprah."

Okay, yes, having everyone stare at you everywhere you went—especially if you were having a particularly fat-feeling day or a ginormous-zit-on-your-forehead day—sounded awful, but still, did she have to take it out on other people?

"Yeah, but I feel like she doesn't even want me here," I confessed.

"Oh, she wants you here—believe me. She told me so," Rose said. "She just need to get used to it, that's all." She sighed as she reached for a plantain. "You see, even with so many people around her all the time, that girl has been alone for a long time. Ever since her mama died. You just need to give it time, baby. She'll come around—don't you worry. Believe me, I know about these kinds of things."

I sure hoped she and Pete were right about all these things they thought they knew.

"Okay, you got your backpack?" Pete asked me. Mom and I were in the lobby, ready to head off to school. Because my school was only ten blocks away on Eighty-fifth and Columbus, we had agreed I could walk there by myself (we even did a few practice runs so I didn't get lost), but for the first day Mom would come with me.

I nodded.

"You got your iPod?"

I nodded again. According to him, even if I didn't have it on, just having the earbuds in my ears would help cut down on the number of crazy people who tried to talk to me as I was walking down the street.

"Phone?"

I held it up for him to see. Since getting lost that first time, I made sure I never left home without it. In fact,

I had Post-its up next to my bedroom door and the front door that read: DID YOU REMEMBER TO TAKE YOUR PHONE?

"You got my number in there in case you run into any trouble or need to know where to find something, right?"

I nodded. Not only did Pete give me all sorts of Dr. Maudelike psychological advice (someone had to, seeing that she still hadn't answered any of my e-mails), but he was like a walking, talking *Guide to New York City* book. If you ever needed to know where the best pizza was (V&T on Amsterdam and 110th) or how to get to the greenmarket in Union Square (go to Seventy-second Street and take the 2 or 3 downtown to Times Square, then switch to the N, R, or Q going downtown to Union Square), Pete was your guy. Plus, when he found out how much I loved cupcakes, he asked around and discovered that Billy's Bakery on Ninth Avenue between Twenty-first and Twenty-second was the best place in the city.

And with his help, I had convinced Mom and Alan to get me my own subway pass. I even passed the quiz Alan had made up about how to get to different parts of the city, and was planning on putting that knowledge to use as soon as I could. It made me sad that I didn't have a friend to go anywhere with yet—like how Rachel, Missy, and I used to go to the mall. But I was hoping that not everyone in my new class would be as unfriendly as Beatrice, or as standoffish as Laurel. Maybe by the end of the week I'd have someone to go with. I was starting to get so lonely, I was even missing Marissa.

"And you're gonna walk into that school with your head held high and just be yourself 'cause you know that that self of yours just happens to be *muy fabuloso*, right?"

I nodded again, but I was lying. I totally didn't feel *muy fabuloso*. I felt *muy* scared.

He patted my cheek. "Okay, *chica*, then you're all set. When I was prayin' this morning, I put in a special request to God to ask that He made it so you make lots of good friends by lunchtime so you didn't have to worry about where to sit."

I gave what I hoped was a brave smile. I guess it wasn't so brave because then he said, "Don't worry—it's going to be fine. Believe me, I'm a doorman. I know about these things."

As Mom and I walked into the Center for Creative Learning, I was very glad that (a) I was wearing a maxipad and (b) I wasn't wearing white pants. I was sure that I was about to get my period any moment on account of how nervous I was. But even getting my period while I was wearing white pants and not wearing a pad wouldn't have been half as horrible as having to stand in front of a roomful of complete strangers while Dr. Margaret Remington-Wallace, my new principal, announced, "Class, I'd like you to say hello to your new classmate, Lucy Parker, who has just moved here from Northampton, Massachusetts." There wasn't a single smile from any of the kids looking back at me except for Beatrice, and even then, hers was just kind of a half smile, not a full one. Instead, I got a roomful of bored stares, except for one boy who did something so gross with his tongue that, if I wasn't the New Girl, I totally would've said, "Ewww...that is sooooo disgusting." Not even Ms. Morgan, the teacher, seemed all that interested in me. She was busy sneaking a peek at her BlackBerry.

"So, Lucy, is there anything you'd like to tell us about yourself before class resumes?" Dr. Remington-Wallace asked. "Here at the Center for Creative Learning, we're all about communication and sharing our feelings."

How about, I totally feel like I'm getting my period right now, so can someone tell me where the bathroom is? Mom had originally wanted to send me to public school, but according to Alan, most of the public schools in Manhattan have metal detectors to make sure the kids don't bring guns inside. She agreed to let me go to private school, but she insisted it not be a snooty one like the ones they showed on those shows Marissa watched on TV. Instead, she put me in a place where, on the brochure, it talked a lot about how the students' "inner artists" came out. Which, if you asked me, didn't seem like a very good fit for someone who wasn't good at art.

You would've thought that a roomful of inner artists would've dressed in cool clothes and the boys would have had long hair, but instead, most of the girls were wearing black and the boys were all preppy, with rugby shirts and Izods. And when I looked at their feet, only one kid had Converses on.

I tried to think of something really funny or smart to say, but because I was so nervous all that came out was, "Um, what time is lunch?"

The morning didn't get any better. Not only did no one talk to me, but I discovered that mixed fractions weren't just a Massachusetts thing. Unfortunately, they had them in New York City, too. And Ms. Morgan called me up to the board to do a problem. And I tripped on my sneaker lace when I was walking up there and almost wiped out.

I don't know why I had asked when lunch was. Not one girl had said, "Hey, since you're new and have no one to sit with, do you want to sit with me at lunch?" So right before lunch period started, I went up to Beatrice and said nervously, "Hi. Remember me? Lucy. We met the other day? I live in your building? And, uh, I was wondering whether you wanted to possibly eat lunch together?" But she said, "Can't. I'm spending it practicing piano in the music room." I was right—she was one of those kids who was totally different in front of adults than she was in front of kids, because there was no real politeness in her tone this time. Instead, she was kind of gruff. Pete had told me a few days earlier that gruff was the New York version of friendly, but that wasn't very comforting when you're feeling completely alone. I had no reason to think that Beatrice was lying, but I still felt like an idiot.

By that time everyone was on their way to the cafeteria, so instead of following them, I did what Laurel did at school and ducked into the girls' room. (At least, as my soon-to-be older sister, she had taught me something worthwhile.) I hung out in one of the stalls until I heard the bell ring. Because the school was kind of fancy, the stall was very clean, which was nice, I guess. There's no way I could have spent an entire half hour in the bathroom at Jefferson without wanting to throw up. Just thinking about Jefferson made me feel even worse, and I couldn't help it when the tears started. Luckily, the toilet paper here was a lot softer than it was at Jefferson, which was good because I had forgotten my Kleenex. As soon as I got home I was going to make DID YOU REMEMBER TO TAKE YOUR KLEENEX? Post-its and put them next to the phone ones, because I had a feeling that I was going to be using a lot of tissues.

chapter 13

Dear Dr. Maude,

By any chance are you familiar with the book *Alexander and the Terrible, Horrible, No Good, Very Bad Day*? It's a kid's book, but I looked online and it was published in 1972, which is why I thought you might know it. Anyway, in case you don't, it's about this boy who has a day that starts out bad and just gets worse and worse. Well, if I wrote a book, it would have to be called *Lucy and the Terrible, Most Awful Week (And It's Not Even Over Yet)*.

I'm totally serious about the "most awful" part. I won't go into all of it because it's kind of a long story, but basically: (a) I hate my new school; (b) I'm totally homesick for everything about Northampton, even Marissa; and (c) Laurel would rather read in her room with the door closed than hang out with me. Oh, and (d) you won't write me back, so I don't know what to do.

Because of all this, I'm seriously considering taking the money I have saved up ($77.29) and getting a bus ticket to Northampton. I looked online and a one-way ticket only costs $39, which means not only would I have enough money to take a cab to Port Authority (even though I passed Alan's subway

194

test, I'm afraid if I take the subway I might get lost and miss my bus), but I'd also be able to buy a sandwich and snacks for the ride. I know if I was a guest on your show, you'd probably say, "Now, Lucy, it sounds to me like you're running away from your problems," and, yeah, I probably am, but I don't care. Just like I don't care that I'll probably get grounded for at least a month, because I can tell you this much—I'd rather be cooped up inside my dad's apartment, where at least I know my way around town and have friends, than on the twenty-first floor of an apartment building full of snooty people and a girl who has no interest in being sisters with me.

I know that by writing you this in an e-mail, you could ruin it by calling my mother and telling her my plan, but I don't think that will happen because—not to be rude or anything—I don't think you even READ my emails. I think you just delete them without opening them, because if you DID read them, then you'd know I was someone who had very serious problems and therefore needed serious advice.

Anyway, I'm not a quitter, and so I have promised myself that I'll finish out the school week and run away on Saturday, which means that, because it's Tuesday, you have three days to write me back. Just as an FYI, if you DON'T write me back, you can consider this is the last e-mail you'll ever receive from me.

I look forward to hearing from you.

yours truly,
LUCY B. PARKER

It would've been nice to have a mother to talk to about the fact that she had ruined my life by yanking me out of my life as I knew it and plopping me down into a new one just because she had gone ahead and fallen in love, but unfortunately, mine was too busy looking for a place to get married, even though they hadn't even decided on a date. I don't know why she was being so crazy about the whole wedding thing when it was only going to be me, her, Alan, and Laurel (well, if my running-away plan went off without a hitch, it would just be the three of them), but she was. I tried to talk to Pete about how miserable I was, but he just kept giving me that "Don't worry, it's going to fine, you just have to give it time" speech, which, frankly, was starting to annoy me. I had given it time—three days—and it only got more awful.

On Wednesday, I was all set to hang out in the bathroom again at lunchtime—especially since I had managed to smuggle two granola bars, a pear, and a rice pudding out of the kitchen that morning when Mom was busy Googling "romantic inns to get married in Vermont in" on her laptop—but that morning during announcements, Ms. Morgan told us that we'd be eating in our classrooms that day because they were painting the cafeteria. I spent the whole morning freaking out about what I was going to do because even though no one showed any interest in me, if someone happened to notice I was gone the entire lunch period and said, "Where were you?" and I said, "Oh, I was in the bathroom," she might think I had really bad stomach problems, and I didn't want to be the New Girl with Stomach Problems. But then, during math, Alice Mosher tapped me on the shoulder and asked me if I wanted to sit with her, and I said yes. I had already figured out that Alice Mosher was the Marissa of the sixth grade, and had no friends, which is why she asked me—the New Girl—to sit with her. She probably thought I was dumb enough not to know any better. I may have been a lot of things, but when it came to figuring out who was who in a class— the Marissa; the Smartest; the One Who Had Probably Kissed at Least Three Boys by Now—I was not dumb. In fact, I had figured that all out by lunch the first day.

It turned out that Alice was even more annoying than Marissa, which I had no idea was even possible. Not only did she talk with her mouth full (if a person is eating a tuna sandwich, that's really disgusting), but because she was deaf in one ear she talked really loud. And she went on and on about how in love she was with Max Rummel, and how, when he said, "Get away from me, you freak, or else I'm going to tell everyone how you're stalking me," what he really meant was, "I'm totally in love with you, too, but I'm afraid all my guy friends will make fun of me if I tell them, so I'm just going to keep being a jerk, but you and I know it's all just an act and I'm totally going to ask you to the seventh-grade dance next year." I didn't mind so much that she talked about herself for most of lunch, because at least I wasn't eating in the bathroom, or becoming the New Girl with Stomach Problems. Plus, I was a little worried about what I was going to say when someone finally asked me about my family, or found out about Laurel. My plan was to not mention Laurel for a while. Like, say, FOREVER. Because I knew once that news got out, I could forget about being Lucy B. Parker, and I'd just be Lucy-Laurel-Moses's-Younger-Stepsister. But it wasn't like I had too much to worry about anyway. It's not like anyone was fighting to sit next to me and ask me all about my life or anything.

Once Alice was done with her sandwich and had moved on to her chocolate pudding, she said—loudly, of course—"So can I ask you something?"

"Uh...sure," I said nervously, hoping this wasn't the moment the stepsister thing came up because I hadn't yet figured out a lie I was happy with.

She leaned in. "Have you gotten your period yet?" she whispered loudly.

Wow. New Yorkers may not have been very chatty, but when they did talk to you, they asked really personal questions. "Um, no," I replied. "Have you?"

She shook her head and sighed. "No. But I'm just dying to. Even though Maren—she's my older sister—says that I won't be all that excited once it's happening every month."

"How many girls in the sixth grade here have gotten theirs?" I asked.

She shrugged. "Fifteen? Twenty? I have no idea."

"You mean no one's keeping track of it?"

"Huh?" she asked, confused.

When I told her about "The Official Period Log of Sixth-Grade Girls at Jefferson Middle School in Northampton, MA" notebook and how I had been the Official Keeper of the Periods, she thought it was the most brilliant idea in the entire world. So brilliant, in fact, that she got up from her seat right then and ran over to where Cristina Pollock, the most popular girl in the sixth grade, and her two BFFs, Chloe and Marni, were sitting and said IN THE LOUDEST VOICE IMAGINABLE, "You guys! You guys! You have to hear this! You know Lucy, that New Girl? Well, back in Maine, where she lived, she was what they called the Official Keeper of the Periods, and she wrote down the dates and times that every girl in the grade got her period so anytime anyone wanted to know that information, they just went to her and she looked in her notebook. Isn't that SUCH a good idea?! Don't you think we should have a notebook like that here at the Center?!"

Not only did the most popular girl in the entire class and her two BFFs all turn to look at me at that moment, but so did everyone who had heard Alice. Which, because she was so loud, was basically everyone in the entire class. Including the boys.

I had to save this. I had to come up with something to say that would make them laugh or at least make them not think I was a total freak who was obsessed with periods. Otherwise, I was definitely going to have to run away on Saturday.

I opened my mouth. "Actually, uh, it's Massachusetts," I stammered.

"Huh?" asked Alice.

"Where I'm from. Not Maine." So much for saving this. I just hoped whoever ended up sitting next to me on the bus didn't smell.

After lunch, I knew I could forget about going to Billy's with a new friend, which was really depressing. Especially because when I'm depressed, the only thing that undepresses me is cupcakes. So when school was over that day, I called Mom and lied and told her that I was going to hang out with a friend ("See, honey—I told you you'd make friends!" she cried), and that I'd be home by dinner, but, really, what I was going to do was take the subway down to Billy's Bakery by myself and get as many cupcakes as I could for $10.28, which was how much money I had in my pocket. Since I was now definitely leaving for good on Saturday, I figured I should at least see if what Pete said was true and they were the best cupcakes not just in Manhattan but the entire world. Plus, it was only fair that I have one good memory of New York City before I went.

Except the problem was I had forgotten my little "Places Pete Says Are Good and What Trains to Take to

Get There" notebook. Luckily I remembered that Billy's was on Ninth Avenue in a neighborhood called Chelsea, so I figured once I got to the subway stop I'd be able to read the map there and just figure it out myself. But when I did get to the subway stop at Eighty-sixth Street, someone had spray painted over the map on the wall there, so I couldn't read it. And the little subway booth, which was supposed to have a live person there to help you out with these kinds of questions, was empty. And then I decided to depend on my memory (which wasn't all that good, especially since it was crammed with all the directions Alan had shoved in it over the last two weeks) about which subway to take. Not a good idea.

I was right about the first part of the trip—taking the 1 train downtown. But that was the only part I was right about. Instead of just taking it down to Twenty-third Street and getting off there and walking west to Ninth Avenue, and then turning left and walking one and a half blocks to Billy's, I got off the train at Forty-second Street. And switched to the N train. But not the N train downtown, which I could have done and not been too messed up. No, I took the N train uptown. And the N train is an express train and therefore makes fewer stops, so I was on it for a while before I noticed something was wrong. "Excuse me," I finally said to the woman sitting next to me when we got to the next stop, "since this is Thirtieth Avenue, I would get off at the next one if I wanted to go to Twenty-third Street in Chelsea, right?"

"Chelsea?!" she replied. "Girl, you on the wrong train. We're in Queens."

Queens?! Queens wasn't even in Manhattan. It was a whole other borough! It was where Pete lived and where Laurel shot her TV show.

The doors *ding-dong*ed and started to close. "Wait!" I yelled as I flew out of my seat. But before I could get off the train, the doors closed and the train took off again.

This was not good. In fact, this was very, very bad. I was lost, in the middle of Queens, and had no idea how to get home.

I got off at the next stop, Astoria Boulevard. If it had been one of Pete's days off, I wouldn't have been so worried, because he lived in Astoria and could've come gotten me. But it wasn't, and he was back in Manhattan at the Conran. I walked out of the subway station and looked around. If I hadn't been completely panicked because I was totally lost, I bet I would've found the whole thing really cool. Astoria Boulevard was swarming with people of all different colors and nationalities, speaking tons of different languages. It was like that "It's a Small World" ride at Disney World, except with real people instead of mechanical ones. But because I was completely panicked and totally lost, I just felt like I was going to collapse.

Thankfully, I had my phone with me. Except when I called Mom to tell her what had happened and that she needed to come get me that very minute, I got her voice mail. So I called Alan, and got his voice mail. And Pete's. And Rose's.

I heard a rumble and looked up. The already-dark sky got darker and a crack of lightning appeared, followed by rain. Which mixed together well with the tears that were already falling down my face. I looked around for someplace dry, and ducked into the Neptune Diner, scrolling through the numbers in my phone. There was only one other person I knew in New York to call and while I totally didn't want to call her, I had no choice.

Laurel. I highlighted her number and, with a deep breath, pressed Send.

"Hello?" a voice on the other end finally said.

"Laurel?" I sniffled. "It's Lucy. I'm really lost," I managed to get out before I burst into tears again.

Ten minutes later, as I was finishing the bowl of clam chowder that Nia, the lady who owned the diner, had made me eat because, according to her, soup fixed everything, a fancy black car with tinted windows pulled up outside and Laurel jumped out, dressed in a clown outfit. Complete with clown makeup.

Just seeing her made me burst into tears again, which was really embarrassing, but I couldn't help it. And then when she rushed into the diner and grabbed me and said, all relieved, "Oh my God, I'm so glad you're okay!" before pulling me into a giant hug, I cried even harder.

Once she let me go, I realized my tears had ruined her makeup. "I made your smile all lopsided!" I cried.

"It's okay," she said. "The whole thing is totally stupid anyway. I kept telling the director that Madison would never dress up like a clown to try and sneak into a famous actor's hotel room, but he forced me to do it." She looked down at her oversized clown shoes. "I must look like a total idiot, though, huh?"

"Not really," I lied.

She took my hand and marched us back over to my booth. "Now tell me what happened. How did you end up in Queens?"

"Well, it's kind of a long story," I said.

"That's okay."

I took a deep breath and told her everything. Not just about how I screwed up on which train to take to Billy's but about everything. How I was sick of getting lost. How no one was nice to me at school. How I was now known in my class as Period Girl, which was a million times worse than New Girl. How my head hurt with trying to remember all the directions and what buttons to push on the remote. How I was trying to be as neat as possible because I knew how important that was to her, but that, unfortunately, I was just a messy person because my parents were creative types.

"And so after school, I decided I'd go to Billy's Bakery to get a cupcake, because Pete says they're the best in the city and I wanted to try one before I left," I sniffled.

"What do you mean, 'left'?" Laurel said. "Where are you going?"

"I'm going back to Northampton," I replied.

"For the weekend?" she asked, confused.

"No. For good."

She was the most confused-looking clown I had ever seen. "What are you talking about?"

"It's just . . . well, I know you told Alan that you were okay with him marrying my mom, but I don't really think you want me here." I couldn't stop the words from coming out of my mouth. "And I just think it would be easier if I went and lived with my dad."

"What? Of course I want you here!"

"Well, you sure don't act like it," I said, twisting my napkin in my hands as I bit the inside of my cheek to stop more tears from coming.

"Well, you don't act like you want me here either!" she said. "Ever since I got home from L.A. you've totally avoided me."

"That's because you've been avoiding me!" I cried.

After we stared at each other for a second, she took a breath and then told me everything—how, after that day at the mall, she had written in her journal how it had been the most fun she had had in she couldn't remember how long. But then, when Alan came back from New York and told her he wanted to marry my mom, she got scared because, while my dad was still alive and I'd always have him, her mom was dead. And what if Alan getting married meant that it completely erased the memory of her mother? Sure, she thought my mom was totally cool, but she felt guilty for moving on and potentially forgetting about her mom. And, yes, she may have been a star, but the truth was she was kind of jealous of how funny and brave I was. And what would happen when, after living with her, I found out that she wasn't the Laurel-Moses-Superstar whom everyone thought they knew but, really, was just this dorky girl who had never played Truth or Dare and whose OCD was so bad that the only way she could make the pit in her stomach go away was if everything was neat and orderly?

I couldn't believe it. Laurel Moses was just as nervous and scared about this whole stepsister thing as I was. Who knew?

"You think I'm funny and brave?" I asked tentatively.

"Yeah, and I know you haven't made any friends yet, but you totally will and then you definitely won't need me," she said.

"Of course I will!" I said. "Like, what am I going to do when I finally get a crush on a boy? Everyone knows that you go to your big sister for that stuff."

"But I've never had a boyfriend," she said.

"Madison Tennyson has."

"I guess you're right." Her eyes got all teary. "I'm really sorry, Lucy. Can we just, I don't know, start over?"

I got teary, too. Again. "Totally," I said, reaching over the table and giving her a hug.

After we let go, I looked at her. "You've really never played Truth or Dare?" I said.

She shook her head.

"Wow. Well, if you want, we can play this weekend. I mean, that is, if you want to hang out."

She nodded. "I want to. So you're not going to go to Northampton?"

I shrugged. "Not yet. I guess I can give the New York thing a little more of a chance."

Laurel had to go back to work, but she lent me her car to take me home. On the way back, I called Mom and told her how I ended up in Queens, and man, was she mad. Like really mad. Like smoke-coming-out-of-a-cartoon-character's-ears-level mad. But then, later at dinner, after she saw how Laurel and I had stopped pretending the other didn't exist and were actually talking, she was glad. Like really glad. So it all evened out, and I didn't even get grounded, which was good.

Of course, I still had to go to back to school the next day. I thought about hiding out in the bathroom again during lunch, but then I remembered what Laurel had said—how I was brave. I still didn't quite buy it. But when I thought about everything that had happened over the last few months—getting dumped by Rachel and Missy; the Hat Incident, half of Northampton seeing my egghead outside the bookstore; embarrassing myself during karaoke; moving away from the only home I'd ever known, and starting at a new school in the middle of the year; living with the most popular girl in the world—well, getting through all of that without dying of embarrassment or melting into the floor might mean I was pretty brave. And if I could do all that, I could sit in the cafeteria like everyone else, even if I sat alone. Because there was no way I was suffering through another lunch with Alice.

But I didn't realize until right before lunch started that, because I hadn't been to the cafeteria yet, I didn't know who sat where.

I was halfway into the ham-and-cheese-on-sourdough-with-balsamic-vinegar-on-top sandwich I had brought from home when Cristina Pollock walked up to my table with her tray, and her two best friends, Chloe and Marni, trailing behind her.

"Hi," she said with a big smile.

I waited for her to add "Period Girl," but she didn't. So instead, I turned around to see who she was talking to, but there was no one there. "Are you talking to me? I asked.

She laughed. "Of course I'm talking to you! It's Lucy, right?"

I nodded. I couldn't believe the most popular girl in the grade was talking to me. Maybe Laurel was right— maybe New York wasn't so bad if you gave it a chance! "Yup. Lucy B. Parker."

"I'm Cristina," she replied. Her smile got a little smaller. "So because you're the New Girl, I guess you didn't know this was my table."

"Uh...no...I didn't—"

"A table where I sit with my friends," she said, motioning to Chloe and Marni. "You know, girls who don't do things like keep notebooks with when everyone gets their periods, and aren't freaks."

Chloe and Marni giggled.

This was it. I could feel my face getting hot. Sure, maybe things were a little better with Laurel and me, but there was no way I could continue coming to the Center anymore. I was brave, but I wasn't *that* brave. Unless a miracle happened in the next twenty seconds, I was going to have to force Mom to homeschool me.

And then I heard it. A miracle.

"At least she's not bourgeois, Cristina," a voice said behind me.

I turned around to see Beatrice standing there, sounding not just gruff but definitely unpolite. I didn't know what *bourgeois* meant, but I could tell from the way she said it, it wasn't a good thing to be.

"Whatever, Beatrice," Cristina said with an eye roll. She turned to me. "So, are you going to move or what, Period Girl?"

I had two choices: be a wimp and get up and go hide in the bathroom again, or stand up for myself and make an enemy for life. The truth was, after everything that had happened over the last two weeks, the standing-up option sounded exhausting. But I wasn't alone anymore.

"Actually, she's eating lunch with me," Beatrice said. "She didn't know that I usually sit in the corner." She turned to me. "Are you coming, Lucy?"

I was so grateful I wanted to hug her, but instead, I just nodded, picked up my stuff, walked across the cafeteria, and had lunch with my first nondoorman, nonhousekeeper friend in New York.

Beatrice Lerner-Moskovitz may have been quiet and polite in front of adults, but once you were alone with her, you couldn't shut her up. By the time lunch was over, I had learned that she lived with her two mothers and thirteen-year-old brother, Blair; that when she grew up, she was going to write novels that won lots of awards; and that when she did, she was going to live in Paris because there weren't as many bourgeois people there.

By this time Alice had joined us, which was sort of annoying. But she got less annoying after she offered me half of her Twix bar. Half of a Twix bar can solve a lot of problems. "I don't mean to sound dumb or anything," I said as I took a bite, "but what does *bourgeois* mean? People don't use that word in Northampton."

Beatrice finished swallowing a bite of her sardine sandwich. "It's hard to explain," she said. "You just sort of know it when you see it. One of my moms uses the word a lot." She patted her mouth with a napkin. "It's French," she added, as if that explained everything.

She went on to tell me that the reason she ate alone was not only because people were grossed out by the fact that she ate sardine sandwiches a lot (it was pretty stinky) but also because, a week before sixth grade started, Cristina—who had been her BFF—called her up and dumped her.

Oh. My. God. I couldn't believe how much we had in common. Not only did we live in the same building, but we had both been dumped!

"It was so dramatic!" cried Alice. "They went from being like Siamese twins to not talking at all."

"Cristina thinks that just because she looks like Laurel Moses, she's God's gift to the universe," Beatrice said. "Personally, I don't think she looks like her, but you'd know better, seeing that you live with her."

Uh-oh. I wasn't ready to drop the Laurel Moses bomb yet. Maybe if I was lucky, Alice had missed that last part because of the deaf-in-one-ear thing.

No such luck. "What do you mean 'seeing that you live with her'?" Alice asked.

"Lucy lives with Laurel Moses," Beatrice explained. "They're about to become stepsisters."

Alice stood up. "Laurel Moses is your stepsister?!" she yelled.

As a cafeteria full of heads whipped around to look

at me, I slumped down in my chair. So much for keeping the Laurel thing a secret.

At least I wasn't the New Girl anymore. Or Period Girl.

Now I was just Laurel Moses's stepsister.

By the time the day ended, I had gotten five notes passed to me from different girls asking me if I wanted to hang out over the weekend, but I already had plans. With Laurel. In addition to playing Truth or Dare, we were going for manicures/pedicures at a place on Columbus Avenue.

But first I was going to meet her at Billy's for a cupcake.

As the last bell rang and we gathered up our stuff, Beatrice came over to me.

"Want to walk home together?" she asked.

"I'd love to, but I can't. I'm going to meet Laurel at Billy's Bakery for cupcakes," I said.

"Oh. Okay. I guess I'll see you around, then," she said as she started to walk away.

"Wait—do you want to come with us?" I quickly called out.

She turned around. "Really?"

I nodded.

Her smile was so big I was almost blinded by the glint off the metal of her braces. "I love Billy's. They have the best cupcakes in all of New York."

I guess Pete did know what he was talking about. As

we started walking to the door, I stopped. "Do you know which subway to take there?" I asked anxiously.

"Of course I do," she replied. "But let's take the bus. The subway is very bourgeois."

"Okay." I shrugged. As long as we didn't end up in Queens, I didn't care how we got there.

"Dr. Maude says that if more New Yorkers took the bus rather than spending so many hours smooshed up against other people in the subway, there'd be a lot less fighting in the world," she said.

"You watch Dr. Maude, too?!" I gasped.

"No. She said it once when I was in the elevator with her."

"What elevator?"

"Our elevator at the Conran. You know she lives in our building, right?"

Dr. Maude was my neighbor?! Like not we-both-live-in-New-York-City kind of neighbors, but in-the-same-building neighbor?!

New York City had just gotten a little bit more interesting.

chapter 14

Dear Dr. Maude,

I'm writing this on what has definitely, positively been the best day I've had in New York since I've lived here, which, because you're a psychologist and your job is to help people get happy, I'm sure makes you very glad to hear.

I won't go into all of it because it's kind of a long story, but basically, here's what you should know:

Laurel and I had this whole long talk, and I'm thinking this stepsister thing might just work out.

I finally have a friend at school—her name is Beatrice Lerner-Moskovitz, and she uses the word *bourgeois* a lot.

If you're ever in the mood for a cupcake, definitely go to Billy's Bakery down in Chelsea because they totally rock.

But most important . . .

You probably didn't know this because I send these letters to you via e-mail rather than regular mail with a return address, but according to Beatrice, WE'RE NEIGHBORS!!!!!!! You live in 12F and I live in 21C!!!!!!!

So now you don't have to write me back—now you can just come up and knock on my door and we can take Id and Ego for a walk in Central Park.

Anyway, I'm going to end this now, because it turns out that once you've had an awesome day after a string of really horrible ones, it takes a lot out of you. I don't think I need any advice at the moment, but I have a feeling I sure will soon, so I'll be in touch then.

yours truly,
Lucy B. Parker

When I'm not busy overlistening to my mom's conversations or being the Official Keeper of the Periods at Jefferson Middle School, I'm updating my website!

LUCYBParKer.com

Check out my site for:

- A sneak peek at upcoming books

- My personal "Why Me?" diary

- The purr-fectly funny "As Seen by Miss Piggy" feature

- Author Robin Palmer's advice column (She's a LOT better at responding than Dr. Maude!)

- Fun downloadables and more exclusive content!